DOLPHIN
KEY

Other Books by Jon Land

JON LAND

DOLPHIN
KEY

A TOM DOHERTY ASSOCIATES BOOK
NEW YORK

DOLPHIN KEY

Copyright © 1999 by Jon Land

A Forge Book
Published by Tom Doherty Associates, LLC
175 Fifth Avenue
New York, NY 10010

Forge® is a registered trademark of Tom Doherty Associates, LLC.

ISBN 0-312-87249-6

First Edition: November 1999

Printed in the United States of America

0 9 8 7 6 5 4 3 2 1

For the miraculous staffs of
Dolphin Human Therapy at Dolphin Cove
and
The Clearwater Marine Aquarium:
Thanks for the rescue!

ACKNOWLEDGMENTS

Thanks to . . .

Natalia Aponte for giving me the idea over lunch at Bolo, for her patience and persistence, and for being the best editor in the world.

Toni Mendez for always being there through thick and thin.

Tom Doherty, Linda Quinton, and the whole Tor/Forge family for believing.

Ann Maurer for refusing to accept anything less than my best.

Scott Swaim and Marianne Klingel of the Clearwater Marine Aquarium for opening the door.

Dr. David Nathanson, the founder of Dolphin Human Therapy, for his genius and hospitality at Dolphin Cove in Key Largo.

Stephen Feinstein for his expertise on Key Biscayne and Virginia Key (all errors, of course, are mine).

David Schechter for his expertise in the law (again, all errors are mine).

Irv and Josh Schechter for their support and encouragement and for never giving up.

Colin Burgess and Andy Stearns for help with the location scouting that ended with the Great Smoke Storm of '99.

And, finally, Sunset Sam, Nikki, Alphonse, Duke, Jeannie, Spunky, and especially Dreamer for putting up with me watching them work.

Of all land animals, some avoid man, and some of those who approach him, like the dog, the horse or the elephant, are loving to him because he feeds them. But on the dolphin, alone among all others, nature has bestowed this gift which the greatest philosophers long for: disinterested friendship. It has no need of any man, yet is the friend of all men, and has often given them great aid.

Plutarch, *On the Intelligence of Animals*

ONE

CHAPTER ONE

"Do I get to swim with the dolphins today?" Zachary Haas asked, his bright blue eyes shining with excitement as he looked up from his wheelchair at Mike Fontana.

Mike crouched down even with Zach. "Absolutely."

The boy's wheelchair was parked at the edge of the dolphin pen forged out of the waters around Key Biscayne. Humidity soaked the air and sunshine sparkled off the ripples made by the swiftly moving dolphins, their slick torsos shimmering when they surfaced to breathe.

"Got to feed them first, though," Zach said, and lowered himself out of his wheelchair. A form of meningitis had taken all four of the boy's limbs, leaving stumps where his arms and legs should have been.

Still in a crouch, Mike eased a bucket of fish over Zach's shoulder. The boy crimped his neck to hold tight to the handle and started forward onto a dock left over from the years when Dolphin Key had been a marina. A lagoon now rested where Key Biscayne residents had once stored their boats in private slips before Hurricane Andrew had struck the island in 1992. Fences extending all the way to the bottom rose three feet out of the water, joining a trio of man-made jetties in isolating the pair of dolphin pens. Three lime-colored buildings with peeling paint stood fifty yards from the grassy shoreline, up a slight natural hillside.

"I hope he's hungry," Zach said, propelling himself along on his stumps as Mike kept pace with him.

They reached the end of the dock and Mike lowered Zach to the floating platform where Dolphin Key's head trainer, Gus Anton, was waiting. The boy angled his entire body to the right to ease the bucket off his shoulder onto the wet wood. An intern named Martha Wallick sat down on the dock behind them, notebook in hand, and Mike nodded to Gus, who leaned over and clicked his fingers in the water to call the dolphin over.

Directly across the lagoon, two more morning sessions atop identical platforms had just gotten underway as well, the scene looking very much the same. Trainer, therapist, and dolphin joined in the common goal of helping the child who sat amidst them. The goal might have been the same, but the cases never were. Autism on Platform 1, word and speech recognition on Platform 2, and Zach here on 3.

"Good girl, George," Mike said, as Gus tossed a small herring to the dolphin who had just popped her head above the surface. Then, to Zach, "Your turn."

Zach anchored a pair of tongs between his neck and shoulder and leaned over toward the wet platform surface. Keeping his head cocked to control them, he lowered the tongs into the bucket and snagged a capelin that he promptly lowered over the water. George opened her mouth gratefully and Zach eased up the pressure on the tongs enough to release the fish straight in.

"Bull's-eye!" Mike complimented, and Gus Anton signaled George to spin in the air directly before the boy.

Zach was already stabbing the tongs into the bucket for another fish. He pulled out a squid this time and dropped it tentacles first toward George's mouth. He missed but the dolphin gobbled it from the surface, and Gus signaled George to wave her flipper as she backpedaled in the water.

Zach shifted his shoulders together as if he were clapping, giggling with appreciation. The tongs slipped to the platform in the process, but he quickly retrieved them and plunged them back into the bucket.

"He likes herring best," the boy said, after George swallowed a second and a third he'd plucked out nimbly.

"She," Mike corrected. "Want to throw her a ball next?"

Zach looked at the dolphin, then nodded.

Mike reached behind him and grabbed a light rubber ball out of a milk crate that had been waiting for him on the platform. He pushed backward to widen the distance from Zach and then tossed the ball lightly forward. The boy leaned over and trapped it between his neck and jaw, then twisted his entire body to the right. The ball sailed sideways, hitting the water a foot in front of George.

"Hey," Mike said, beaming, "got it the first time today. Now let's see how you catch."

Before them, George retrieved the ball and tossed it back with a flip of her nose. The ball landed just short of Zach and plopped onto the platform with a small splash. The boy leaned over and squeezed it between his head and shoulder.

"Girls can't throw," he said.

"Not as good as you."

"Can we swim now?"

"You're the boss."

Mike slipped gently into the lagoon first and then eased

Zach in after him. He made sure the boy's yellow life belt was tight and then cradled Zach in against his chest before paddling away from the platform.

"What should we try first?" Mike asked.

"Foot push!"

"You got it," Mike said and leaned back. On the platform Gus fed George a fish and gave her the proper hand signal.

In the next instant, Mike felt the dolphin's powerful nose jam up against his foot and begin to push. Immediately he was being propelled backward through the water, Zach squealing with delight in his arms. George circled them back to the platform where Gus was ready with another snack.

"How about a ball push next?" Mike suggested.

"Good idea!"

"So let's go for it."

"Here it comes," said Martha, the intern, from the platform.

She put her notebook down and tossed the rubber ball out into the water. Mike gave Zach enough slack to crimp his body over and capture it, just as he had on the platform. The boy maneuvered the ball against his chest, and George approached from the front, her nose riding over the water enough to lodge against the ball. Again she pushed her passengers in a circle that ended back at the platform in cadence with a soft chorus of whistle blows from Gus.

"I want to get in the water with George," Zach said, as the dolphin rose eagerly before Gus for another fish.

"You are."

"I mean *swim* in the water with her. For real. On my own. Like other kids."

Mike looked up at Gus, who was glaring at the birds that had gathered atop the railing behind them, waiting to steal whatever fish eluded George. Mike heard him mutter something in German under his breath.

"How about next time?" Mike asked Zach.

"You promise?"

"So long as you're patient with me."

CHAPTER TWO

Back on shore, Mike found Jacardi Benoit standing under a shaded canopy just past the dock.

"I thought we could have lunch today, mombo," Jacardi said, his crossed arms looking like black bands of iron coiled over his chest.

Mike grabbed a towel from the picnic table and draped it around his wet shoulders. "How about take-out from the Oasis?"

Jacardi wrinkled his nose. "That Cuban stuff'll burn a hole in your stomach so big you won't need the one in your ass anymore, mahn."

"You get what you pay for."

"Could that be some degree of fiscal responsibility I just heard?"

"No, just bad taste in food. A problem I've got."

Jacardi frowned. "One of many, mombo: I had another look at your books."

"You do that for all your clinical psychology students?"

"Only the ones that got no sense about their money."

Jacardi Benoit had come with his parents from Haiti to Florida in a sailboat before the practice became commonplace.

His mother was a voodoo princess who painted his forehead with chicken blood every night to chase away the evil spirits she was afraid might follow the family to their new land. Jacardi had learned to speak English and gone on to graduate from high school and then college. His mother credited the chicken blood, and Jacardi, who was every bit as tall as Mike but with muscles that looked sculpted of clay, didn't argue. Later he had become a clinical psychology professor at a local community college, where he met Mike for the first time in class.

Jacardi took off his fisherman's cap and mopped the black dome of his head, which was shiny with sweat. "I think maybe you need to come with me to the old *gris-gris* ladies so they can make a spell, mombo."

"You talking voodoo or accounting?" Mike asked. "Mombo" meant voodoo prince, which Jacardi started calling him after witnessing the kinds of things that went on at Dolphin Key, pretending to credit the results to magic rather than motivation.

"Somebody out there must be sticking pins in a Mike Fontana doll to put you in the mess you're in," said the big Haitian.

"I've got a lousy financial advisor, that's all. Made a string of bad investments."

"What investments, mombo? You sold everything you ever had to keep this place going, including your house. What's your little one think of that?"

"Joe likes it here just fine."

"Doesn't miss having a real roof over his head, does he? Likes living in a shack?"

Jacardi gazed skeptically toward the ramshackle trio of

buildings that rimmed the area above the shoreline. Their clapboard roofs and shingled sides were bleached by the salt and the sun. Inside was the center's equipment, office, and, as of late, home for Mike and his son. A home dwarfed by the endless rows of high-rise condominums that continued to sprout up along Key Biscayne's shoreline. Dolphin Key was located in Bill Baggs State Park, a half mile past the last of the high-rises, around a bend that provided the feeling of a cove and offered a clear view of the Cape Florida Lighthouse.

Mike slapped Jacardi on a shoulder that felt like stripped steel. "That's why I eat Cuban sandwiches at places like the Oasis, big man," he said and headed toward the middle structure.

Jacardi followed him up a wheelchair ramp into the building, where Mike wiped his feet off on a green mat soaking in a tub of fresh water. "This ain't funny, mombo. I've been through the figures and they don't lie. You got to come up with a better way of doing business. You don't charge enough for your sessions, and you give too many scholarhips. You got to become more like the centers in Key Largo. Think about it, mahn."

"I have."

"How many trainers you got on full-time?"

"Five."

"What about therapists?"

"Four right now, including me."

"I don't include you."

"Look, Dolphin Key isn't like the centers in Key Largo, big man."

"No, they're trying to stay in business. You're barely

clearing enough money to feed these creatures of yours. You gonna go hungry, while they're still stuffing their noses." Jacardi held Mike's stare for a moment. "Listen to me. These people who don't pay, they taking slots away from people who can."

"And what happens to the ones who can't?"

"I don't know. Maybe they buy a dog instead. I'm not trying to save them, mombo. I'm trying to save you."

"I'll figure something out."

"Maybe I already have."

Mike tensed, knew what was coming next. "You've been talking to Gus again."

"Told me he doesn't like those birds that've been hanging around. Told me he was going to shoot them."

"Gus tends to exaggerate."

"Know what else he told me? He got this public swim thing all figured out. Therapy sessions in the morning, then the swims in the afternoon. A hundred twenty-five dollars per person and maybe forty, fifty people per day. Do the math."

"You shouldn't be listening to Gus."

"Without him, you wouldn't have this place, mahn, and two of the dolphins are his. I figure that gives him a right to express his opinion. You don't listen and maybe he shoots you instead of the birds that get him so upset."

"And what gives you the right to express *your* opinion?"

"I got a lot invested in you, too. Time instead of money. I don't want to see it go to waste."

"It's not."

"I know you're not listening. But there's something else I've got to say you *need* to listen to . . ."

"It'll have to wait," Mike said and started on again, his feet squishing against the indoor-outdoor carpet.

"But, mombo . . ." Jacardi stopped and snickered.

"Something wrong?"

"That awful fish smell."

"It doesn't bother you when you're eating them."

"That's because I don't have to see the creatures before they're thrown in the pot."

Mike walked ahead of Jacardi into a kitchen area complete with a trio of refrigerators and dual chrome sinks. There was lots of shelving and counter space as well, much of it filled with buckets and pails of all sizes and compositions. Magic marker boards lined the walls, one board for each of the six dolphins, carefully detailing exactly what each ate every single day.

"Hi, Jilly," Mike greeted a little girl standing between a pair of interns near the window. The interns, mostly marine biology students, rotated on a semester basis and were invaluable at Dolphin Key. Mike hesitated to consider how he might otherwise pay for the same services that were good only for class credits and a Dolphin Key T-shirt now.

The seven-year-old girl turned and squirmed shyly.

Mike crouched down in front of her as Jacardi hovered back near the doorway. "You ready to feed the dolphins, buddy? You ready to feed Paul?"

She nodded.

"Okay, let's get Paul's food. Do you remember where it is?"

Jilly hesitated, then nodded before starting off toward the refrigerators.

"She has Williams syndrome," Mike told Jacardi.

"Which means?"

"She has trouble sequencing thoughts, and recalling anything poses a tremendous challenge."

"Why doesn't she have any of the physical abnormalities usually associated with Down's?"

"Because Williams doesn't genetically alter the appearance."

Jacardi nodded from the doorway, impressed. "Looks like I taught you pretty well, mombo."

Jilly stopped in front of the refrigerators.

"We're going to feed Paul today," Mike reminded, kneeling alongside her. "Which refrigerator is Paul's food in?"

Jilly's face tightened in concentration. She squirmed slightly again before moving to the first refrigerator and tugging it open. Inside was a metal bucket of food complete with a name tag taped upon it: PAUL.

"Very good, Jilly!" Mike said and squeezed the little girl's shoulders tenderly. "Now, get Paul's—"

He didn't have to complete the sentence; Jilly had already reached in and grasped the bucket with both hands.

"What do we do next, Jilly?" he asked instead.

The girl's answer was to lug the bucket toward the sink and lower it to the ground. Mike dragged a stool over for her to climb up onto.

"That's right! We've got to wash Paul's fish before we can feed him."

"I really got to talk to you about something else important, mombo," Jacardi said from the doorway as Mike lifted the bucket of fish to the counter and then helped Jilly onto the stool. Before he was ready, she had grabbed a squid from the bucket.

"What's that?" Mike asked her.

She didn't reply, holding the squid out toward the faucet instead.

Mike cupped his hand around hers, as he turned on the water. "Check the temperature. Make sure it's right."

Jilly ran her palm under the water and, satisfied, started the squid toward the faucet.

"What's it called?" Mike asked her again as the water ran over it. "It's a squid, isn't it? It's a squid."

"Squid!" Jilly repeated.

Mike took it from her grasp, so she could reach into the bucket for something else, emerging with a pair of herring this time.

"How many fish?" he asked her.

Jilly was already washing them.

"How many fish, Jilly?" Mike repeated. He touched one of the herring and then the other. "One, two . . . Now, how many fish, Jilly?"

She continued the washing, not seeming to follow. Then, suddenly, she turned toward him.

"Two!"

"That's right! Very good!"

Jacardi shook his head from the doorway. "You the one needs to learn how to count, mombo."

Before Mike could respond, his son, Joe, came dashing into the kitchen. The sleeves of his wet suit dangled by his knees and his sneakers squeaked as he ran, his long hair flying in all directions.

"Crandon Park Beach, Dad!" the boy said. "We got one beached!"

Mike signaled the interns to take his place at the sink with Jilly and turned back toward Jacardi Benoit. "I'll meet you at the truck."

"Me, mahn?"

"There someone else standing there?"

"Why I got to help you save another of these creatures?"

"Because Joe can't drive the truck and I can't spare anyone at the center," Mike said, drawing even with Jacardi. "You coming?"

CHAPTER THREE

"All rise!"

Katy Grant stood up alongside her court-appointed attorney as Judge Celine Rosenthal entered the stifling, dingy courtroom. Rosenthal was a sour-faced woman with a perpetual frown worn into her expression. She was as devoid of emotion as she was of color, the Florida sun having somehow missed her wherever she went. Katy remembered her lawyer saying Rosenthal was as tough as they came. Just the luck of the draw she had been assigned this case instead of the gruff, fatherly sorts who could usually be cajoled into leniency.

As she strode toward the bench, Judge Rosenthal seemed to make a determined effort not to look at Katy. Katy decided at once it was going to be bad, bad as it could be, and she found that she didn't care. She had gone too far to turn back, and there wasn't much good to look at in that direction anyway. A cramped walk-up efficiency in a converted motel closer to Liberty City than the water. The television got one channel, and she could no longer afford even the fifty bucks per week rent after her boyfriend moved out three months before. The bastard had even taken the air conditioner with him, leaving a gaping hole in the wall and sticking Katy with the bill. The only other thing he'd left behind was his checkbook, which

Katy had promptly emptied around town in spite of its zero balance. It was the eighth bad check that had gotten her caught.

Katy ran things over in her head, looked for what she could have done differently. Could she have played up to her probation officer and sung the song he wanted to hear, kissed ass in return for another suspended sentence? A stiff lecture, some community service, and until the next time they brought her in, it was *adios muchachos*. She had known what she had to say, but the words hadn't been there. Hardly a surprise, since she hadn't tried to find them.

Judge Rosenthal tapped her gavel and Katy snickered as she sat back down, drawing a harsh stare from her lawyer.

"The defendant will please rise," the judge said.

Katy rose again with her lawyer by her side. Public defender fresh out of law school named Snead who was always fumbling through manila folders for pages he never seemed to find. She didn't like the way he drew lines up her legs with his eyes. Katy was still getting used to her hair almost reaching her shoulders again, having let her former spiked punk style grow out on the advice of her last public defender. On the advice of this one, she had taken out her eyebrow and nose rings, but not her many earrings, which clearly upset him. Katy was glad she had given Snead something else to look at.

"Ms. Grant," Judge Rosenthal began, "I have reviewed the matter before this court carefully and have reached some difficult conclusions."

Ceiling fans spun lazily overhead, but in the silence that followed the judge's opening remarks, Katy could hear every whir. The Criminal Courts Building was located in the shadow of the old Orange Bowl and Katy knew from experience that the air-conditioning didn't work very well at all.

"The record will show my aversion to the word *incorri-*

gible," Rosenthal continued. "The record will also show my outspokenness on the subject of the failure of our penal system to perform any real and worthwhile rehabilitation. For this reason, I search my soul for leniency, for reasons for compassion and hope." She leaned forward. "But in your case, Ms. Grant, I'm afraid I can find none.

"Starting with the violent offenses you were charged with as a member of the gang known as the Dade Flood while still a juvenile—"

"Your Honor, I must object to—"

"Be quiet, Mr. Snead," Rosenthal snapped at Katy's court-appointed attorney. "I assure you that your client's juvenile records did not figure at all in my decision; if they had, you would have found me even more demonstrative today. Now, as I was saying, Ms. Grant, you have tried the patience of this and other courts again and again over the past five years. This is your fourth conviction during that period, and I no longer see leniency as an option. You have trod upon the court's compassion and besmirched the very notion of probation."

Judge Rosenthal leaned back, her expression like granite.

"I have taken into account your often tragic past. An abusive, alcoholic father running out when you were two. Your mother dying when you were nine." The sympathy faded from her face as quickly as it had appeared. "However, this court must determine the point where the baggage from one's past stops becoming an acceptable rationale for bad behavior in the present. I'm afraid that the level of misfortune that has beset you is not acceptable as an excuse for wanton displays of violence and indiscretion. A line must be drawn, and I am prepared to draw it."

Rosenthal leaned forward over the bench.

"Ms. Grant, it is the decision of this court that your probation be revoked, effective immediately, and that you be re-manded to the custody of the Dade County Correctional Institution, also effective immediately, to serve the balance of the two-year term previously imposed. Bailiff, please take the defendant into custody." The judge tapped her gavel. "We're adjourned."

CHAPTER FOUR

Crandon Park Beach was the most popular in all of Dade County, leading to massive traffic tie-ups coming onto Key Biscayne almost every day of the summer. Coming from the opposite direction down Crandon Park Boulevard, though, Mike had made it to the beach in five minutes flat.

He approached the beached dolphin lying helpless on the wet sand, while Jacardi Benoit stopped well short of it.

"He won't bite," Mike's twelve-year-old son, Joe, said, brushing the long brown hair from his face.

"Not you maybe, little one."

"Come on," Joe urged. "I'll protect you."

"What kind of creature you call this, little one?" Jacardi asked Joe, following reluctantly.

"Atlantic Bottlenose."

"Why he do this to himself?"

"Nobody knows for sure. He might be sick, but sometimes they just get tired and lost, panicked maybe." Joe gave the dolphin a longer look. "I think this one's sick."

The dolphin lay motionless on the sand, baking in the hot sun and eyeing the nearby water as if it were a mile away. Mike approached slowly, making sure the dolphin could see him. No sudden moves that might startle it. The lifeguards had done a good job of keeping the crowds back. One of them was using a children's sand pail to pour water over the stranded creature's body.

The lifeguard backed off when Mike approached and crouched. Then Mike edged closer and sat down in the sand, showing the dolphin his hands. Only after he was sure it had seen him did he reach out and gently stroke the top of its head. Its dehydrated skin had lost its silky sheen, feeling dry and already showing the pinkish lines of sunburn. Only 10 percent of rescued dolphins actually survive the trauma, but Mike always assumed the latest would be that one in ten.

"Okay," Mike said, "I'm gonna stay here and wet him down a little. Jacardi, you go get the truck."

"Get the truck? Why not just put him back in the water, mahn? He looks fine to me."

"They don't beach themselves like this unless there's something wrong. We need to check him out, see if we can get him back to the water another day. Now get the truck, big man. Joe, go with him and get the winch ready."

The boy dashed on ahead of Jacardi, who glared back at Mike, shaking his head.

Minutes later, Joe stood in the rear bed of the truck while Jacardi backed it up to where Mike hovered over the beached dolphin. At once the boy worked the sled attachment down onto the wet sand and jumped in to hold it steady against the determined push of the stiff breeze coming off the ocean. The sled was made of a strong but pliable rubber bed capable of supporting anything up to a thousand pounds. Joe maneuvered it alongside the dolphin and then he and Mike gently rolled the dolphin upon the bed.

Then, with Mike touching the dolphin to comfort him, the boy climbed back into the truck bed and eased the throttle of the winch forward. Instantly the sled began to rise with a grinding sound, slowing when the dolphin's weight settled into it. The angle of the winch drew the sled backward toward the bed as it was raised.

Mike followed, holding the dolphin the whole way. The trickiest part came when it was time to ease the animal down into the truck. Here, Mike had to dance agilely sideways, supporting the sled at the same time he climbed into the truck.

"That's it, Joe," Mike said, when the sled was angled directly over the bed. "Ease him down now."

The sled kissed the truck bed with a soft thud and the dolphin squirmed slightly.

"Easy, boy," Mike soothed. "Easy."

He was reaching for the hose fed by an external water tank that he would use to keep the animal doused all the way back to Dolphin Key when a commotion on the beach drew his attention.

"Who the hell is that, mombo?" Jacardi asked from the cab.

"Trouble," Mike told him.

CHAPTER FIVE

A rail-thin man with baked leather skin pushed his way past the lifeguards' makeshift barricade, heading straight for the surf. Foamy seawater ran over his expensive sport boots and pant cuffs, but he pretended not to notice. He wore a khaki vest over his short-sleeved T-shirt and matching olive-drab cargo pants.

"Trouble?" Jacardi asked Mike.

"His name's Max Hollister and he's probably the most famous dolphin trainer of all time."

"But it sure don't look like he's a friend of yours, mahn."

"You got that right. Hollister had a radical change of heart a few years ago. Doesn't believe any dolphin should be kept in captivity for any reason. It's become an obsession with him, and he's not going to stop until there's not one dolphin left in any center or aquarium."

"Acts like he owns the beach, the bastard."

"He trained dolphins for television, the movies, too."

The odd thing was, Mike didn't totally disagree with Hollister. Watching dolphins leap through hoops or rings of fire in theme parks reduced them to sideshow attractions, which also accounted for Mike resisting the addition of public swims to Dolphin Key. Ironically, Mike's own father had been one of the original animal rights activists, a park ranger in the Everglades who had declared war on poachers thirty years before.

"I don't watch neither, mahn," Jacardi said, as Hollister planted himself squarely in front of the bumper.

"You can keep your truck right here, Mike."

Mike left the task of hosing down the rescued dolphin to Joe and faced Max Hollister from the truck bed.

"Hey, mombo," Jacardi called, "you want me to run him over?"

"No," Mike said, "I think I'd rather watch his shoes get ruined."

Hollister glanced for a moment at Joe hosing water on the dolphin. "Got enough water in that tank to last a lifetime, Mike? Because that's how long I'm going to stand here."

"There's a whole ocean behind me, Max. But Jacardi will run you over a long time before we need it."

Jacardi revved the old truck's engine to punctuate Mike's point.

"Free that dolphin, Mike. Let nature run its course."

"Nature's what stranded him, Max."

"It's the natural order of things and you're getting in the way of it."

"Just like you're getting in my way. Now mind your own goddamn business and stand aside."

A light layer of sweat glistened on Hollister's brow, making his dark face look like burnt oilskin. "I've made it my business to make sure no more dolphins end up imprisoned."

"The dolphins living at Dolphin Key aren't prisoners. Isn't that right, Joe?"

"Damn right," Mike's son said, his lips tightened in a scowl as the cool water from the hose pooled briefly across the rescued dolphin.

Hollister stood a little taller. "The boy's got your manners, Mike."

"I was in Vietnam, Max. You're lucky he doesn't have my gun."

Hollister smiled at that. "Too bad I'm not here on behalf of child welfare. I mean, considering your past."

Mike glared down from the truck bed.

"Come on now, do you really think it's wise for people to be trusting you to take care of their children?"

Mike laid his palms down on the truck's scalding roof. "They trust me because I get results."

Hollister smirked. "Nobody's ever proven this kind of therapy has any effect at all."

"I guess you've never heard of Dr. David Nathanson."

"On the contrary, I'm heading down to his facility in Key Largo tomorrow." Hollister looked proud of himself. "Take it from someone who's been there, Mike—"

"I've never been where you were," Mike interrupted. "I only work with sick and rescued dolphins, and I handle the rehab myself. The ones that the aquariums and theme parks, and trainers like you used to be, don't want."

"You turn them into dime-store attractions, like everybody else. But, don't worry, I'm not one to discriminate: I plan on shutting all of you down." Hollister drummed his fingers on the old truck's hood. "Do you know how many dolphins died in captivity last year? Do you know how many parks keep them in pens too shallow or small to properly swim? Have you seen the petting zoos?"

"How many times you been arrested this year for staging these protests?"

"I know you've lost two dolphins yourself in the past nine months."

"One. The other was transferred to Grassy Key because she needed surgery."

"I won in South Carolina, Mike," Hollister reminded, referring to a recent court decision in that state that banned any public display of dolphins or whales, even those at therapy centers like Dolphin Key. "I'll win here, too."

Mike leaned over the truck bed. "You mind standing aside, Max? I'm starting to lose my patience."

Hollister stuck out his bony chest. "I'll stand aside as soon as that creature is returned to the sea."

"Yup," Mike said, hurdling his bearlike figure down to the sand, "that's what I figured."

Mike watched Hollister flinch as he came forward. He threw open the truck's door and started to climb into the driver's seat.

"Move over," he said to Jacardi.

"Whatever you say, mahn."

Mike revved the engine. "Hold on, Joe," he said, out the window.

Maybe Hollister expected a warning. Maybe he mistook Mike's resolve for bravado. Either way, he was barely able to throw himself out of the way when the old truck lurched forward. Hollister hit the sand hard, and the surf soaked his cargo pants and khaki vest.

The truck tore past him, spitting sand as Hollister climbed back to his feet, seaweed stuck to his vest pocket and his oilskin face spotted with water.

"You like saving things, don't you, mahn?" Jacardi asked him.

"Nothing I enjoy more."

"That's good," Jacardi said, "because you still got your work cut out for you today."

CHAPTER SIX

They put Katy Grant in a holding cell with a crackhead who lay on a naked mattress staring at the ceiling. The wing was surprisingly cool but stank of stale urine and vomit. Katy wondered how long it would take before she grew used to the moaning and retching. She was glad she couldn't see into any of the other cells.

"So how's the food here?" Katy asked her cellmate.

There was no reply.

"That good, eh?"

The woman's eyes continued to watch the ceiling, as if that's where the world was happening. Katy lay down on her back and looked up at the peeling paint and zigzagging cracks, waiting for something else to appear.

She imagined the hot, stale air outside, smelling of cooked tar and gasoline vapors that thickened over engines and outside of tailpipes. The pavement and buildings sucked in the heat like a sponge and squeezed it back out a little at a time. In summer, even close to the water, the breezes felt oven-baked and offered no break from the humidity. If her cell had a window, late in the afternoon she could watch the inevitable grimy rain that fell like bathwater dumped from the sky and turned city sidewalks to steam vents when it landed.

Katy heard the rattle of footsteps outside her cell and looked up to see a guard working his key into the lock.

"You got a visitor," he announced.

Katy pushed herself off the cot. "I don't know anybody."

"Somebody knows you. Come on," he said.

Mike Fontana studied his reflection in the window of the visitor's room door while he waited for Katy Grant to appear. He hadn't looked in the mirror much, as little as possible in fact, for years now, since he stopped liking the person who looked back. He'd broken the last mirror he'd really stared into; in the bathroom at Jimbo's Bar on Virginia Key, just after his second wife dropped by to tell him she was leaving. Mike had given himself a look then, studying the bloodshot eyes and dark curls the humidity had pasted to his scalp.

Today the window glass showed pretty much the same curls, but the red was gone from his eyes, replaced by a paleness that made it look like they'd gone dry in the sockets. He watched Katy Grant walking alongside the guard, the man's free hand hovering instinctively just over the grip of his nightstick.

The guard opened the door and waited for Katy to enter before closing it. She looked around the room, past Mike as if she expected someone else to be there. Then she turned her head to the side, eyeing him quizzically.

"I know you?"

"No. My name's Mike Fontana."

Katy looked down, studying her shoes. "I'm not supposed to have visitors. That means you must pull some weight around here. You my new Johnny Law?"

"I spoke to your probation officer."

"What about?"

"Getting you out of this place."

Katy snickered. "I miss something here?"

"Community service. Six months worth, starting tomorrow."

She put her hands on her hips, eyes looking like gunsights. "What's the catch?"

"You don't get paid. Not even a dime."

"How am I supposed to live?"

"Social Services will pay your rent and basic living expenses."

"Do I get to eat?"

Mike nodded. "And stay out of jail."

"A six-month gig and the two years get eighty-sixed?"

"Screw up with me and you go straight on back to the lockup."

Katy sat down in one of the chairs and put her feet up on the table. "You wouldn't happen to have a cigarette, would you?"

Mike shook his head. "Bad for your health, like jail."

Katy gave the man a longer look. She always compared people to movie stars when she met them, an old habit she'd had since she was a kid, when she imagined that's who the people really were. Coming to adopt her. Mike Fontana was a tough one, though she quickly settled on a sad version of Bruce Willis with hair. He had a young face but old eyes. She put his age in the mid-forties, maybe a couple years either way.

"Sometimes the bad things are the most fun," she said, leaning back.

"And the fun things are what landed you here."

"Lucky for me you showed up when you did."

Mike Fontana tried to ignore her sarcasm, but Katy could

see his expression hardening, lips curling slightly back. "Luck had nothing to do with it. The probation office sends over files on people who fit the criteria for our community-service program."

"Criteria?"

"Offenders for whom prison is mostly likely to have a detrimental effect."

"I never met anyone it had a good effect on."

"Offenders who might benefit more from a different approach, then."

"What's your approach?"

"Ever heard of Dolphin Human Therapy?"

"Hey, they need shrinks, too?"

"Not exactly." Mike took a step toward the door, then stopped. "You interested or not?"

She lowered her feet from the table. "If it gets my reservation here cancelled, you're damn right I am."

Mike nodded. "Then let's go get you checked out."

CHAPTER SEVEN

The boy sat with his legs crossed beneath him on the platform. His thin shoulders slumped forward. His hands hung limply by his sides, fingers held open as if they had forgotten how to close. He rocked slightly from side to side.

According to his parents, eight-year-old Stephen Hatch suffered from a severe case of autism that had kept him from speaking a single word. Dan and Lorraine Hatch watched Stephen's first session from beneath the small canopy just above the shoreline. So far they hadn't seen very much at all. Stephen had cried and screamed through the first twenty minutes of the session before Mike finally got him calmed down.

Mike sat directly in front of the boy on a platform in the slightly smaller pen where a pair of dolphins named Sonny and Cher lived. At Dolphin Key, trainers rotated sessions so the dolphins never worked consecutively: three or four sessions in the larger pen, followed by two in the smaller adjoining pen throughout the day, which always ended by three P.M. to allow time for parent workshops and home visits by the therapists. Head trainer Gus stood behind Mike and to the right, feeding the dolphin named Sonny enough to coax him to stay close to the platform even though the boy seemed utterly uninterested.

"Stephen," Mike tried again. "I want you to listen to me, Stephen."

He tried shifting himself a little closer, but the boy recoiled, flailing his arms defensively. He stopped when he saw Mike wasn't coming any closer.

Mike reached into the milk crate at his side and came out with a pair of plastic squares, one red and one blue. He tapped them together to regain the boy's attention.

"Stephen. Look at me, Stephen. Come on, I know you're listening. I know you can hear me."

The boy peeked out, lifting his head slightly.

"Can you tell me which one of these is blue?"

Stephen seemed to be staring right past him.

Mike held out the red square. "Is this blue, Stephen? Is this blue?"

The boy turned away, crinkling his nose as if he had gotten a whiff of something he didn't like.

Mike held out the blue square instead, where he was sure Stephen could see it. "Is this blue, Stephen? Look at it and touch it if it's blue."

Stephen didn't seem to be looking at all. But suddenly he plucked the blue square from Mike's hand and tossed it into the water. Prompted by Gus, Sonny retrieved the square with his nose and pushed it right up against the platform. Stephen's eyes turned slightly toward the dolphin, who seemed to be looking at him too.

"Thank you, Sonny," Mike said, as he leaned over and picked the square up. "Would you like to touch the dolphin, Stephen?"

When Stephen continued staring at Sonny, Mike gently took the boy's hand and started to lower it toward the water.

Almost instantly Stephen pulled it away and closed himself up into a ball.

"Tactile defensiveness," Mike said to the intern charting the session behind him.

"Resistant to any form of touching," Martha Wallick expounded, as she made her notes.

Stephen was rocking himself again, moaning softly with his head buried between his knees.

Holding a square in either hand again, Mike slid closer so Stephen could see him. "Throw the blue one in the water again, Stephen. Pick the blue square and throw it in the water again."

The boy refused to look up.

Mike laid the squares down on the platform and closed his beefy hands gently on either side of Stephen's head. Again the boy began to wail, trying to pull away, but this time Mike wouldn't let him. He thrashed harder and still Mike wouldn't let him.

"Look at me, Stephen. I want you to look at me. Look at me and I'll let go of you."

Finally the boy met at least some of his gaze and Mike let him go. He retrieved the squares and started again. "All right, pick the blue one out for me."

The boy made no motion to do that, but Mike did see his eyes shift from side to side. Mike reached back into the milk crate for a second blue square to replace the red one. Then he held the squares, both blue now, up again before Stephen.

"Pick the blue one out for me. You don't have to touch it. Just pick it out."

Stephen focused on the square Mike was holding in his right hand, stopping just short of a nod.

"Very good."

Quick as he could, Mike snatched a pair of red squares from the milk crate to replace the blues ones.

"Now, pick the red one out for me. Just like you picked the blue one."

Stephen shifted slightly toward Mike's other hand and almost reached out his hand this time.

"Very good!" Mike said, making sure the boy could hear the pleased tone in his voice. "Sonny's happy you did that, too. Let's see if he can show us how happy."

Behind them Gus gave the dolphin the signal for a jump, and Sonny soared into the air and sliced effortlessly back beneath the surface. Stephen's eyes fluttered, then went down again.

Mike slipped agilely off the platform and leaned his upper body over the edge close to Stephen, while the rest of him was in the lagoon. "Want to go swimming with Sonny, Stephen?"

The boy tightened himself into a ball again, head covered by his hands.

"You don't have to come in, Stephen. But I thought you might want to play with the dolphin."

He was rocking himself now, showing no interest.

"You did your best. Thank you," Lorraine Hatch said, drying her son with a towel as he stood stiffly before her.

"I'm not finished yet," Mike told her.

"We don't want to waste your time, considering we're on scholarship."

"You're not wasting my time. That was only the first session, and it ended a lot better than it started."

"How?"

"He began to respond. His tactile defensiveness lessened a little."

Lorraine Hatch smiled as if she had heard similar words before. "Nothing's going to happen. It never does. We're used to it."

"What my wife is trying to say," her husband interrupted, "is that we don't have a lot of money. You know how much we appreciate the scholarship, but the airfare, rental car, and week in the motel might break us, and that's the absolute truth."

"He's been like this his whole life," Mike said.

Lorraine Hatch swung back toward him. "We told you that."

"Then give us a couple more days, and let's see what happens. See if we can make some progress. If it takes longer than that, I'll take care of your motel room. Agreed?"

The Hatches nodded together, slowly, looking almost embarrassed.

Mike crouched down in front of Stephen. "Same time tomorrow, kid."

CHAPTER EIGHT

"You have trouble finding the place?" Mike asked Katy Grant when she arrived at Dolphin Key the next morning. "I was expecting you an hour ago."

"Yeah," she said, chomping her gum in the parking lot, "well, do both of us a favor and don't expect too much." Already counting down the days, a solid hundred and eighty of them. Hopefully this counted as one.

Mike dragged over a trash can. "I expect you not to chew gum. You can start again by getting rid of it."

She smacked the wad noisily between her teeth. "Why?"

"It's not allowed here. People spit it out on the grass or the docks, and when we wash the place down, it ends up in the pens where the dolphins could eat it and get sick." Mike tilted the trash can toward her. "In here, please."

Katy spit the wad from her mouth and missed the can by three feet. "Oops."

Mike picked up the gum himself and tossed it in the trash. Katy smirked and wedged her hands into the pockets of her jeans. She had given serious thought to going back to her spiked hairstyle, then settled for reclipping rings through her eyebrows and nose to complement her regular assortment of earrings. Ripped jeans, too; enough rips, she hoped, to make Mike Fontana send her home to change.

Mike seemed to notice the rings for the first time. "Interesting taste in jewelry."

"I wanted to look my best."

"How much do you know about what happens at Dolphin Key?"

"Well, I know you're not allowed to chew gum."

"Okay," Mike told her, "let me lay it out for you. What we do, in a nutshell, is help children. Lots of them come here because they've got nowhere else to turn. Maybe their parents have tried other places and they aren't any better off for it. Maybe those other places told them not to bother. So the children come here, from all over the world, and more often than not they leave a lot better off than when they came in."

"Like who?" Katy wondered.

"I'll show you."

Mike led her down to the shoreline overlooking the two seawater dolphin pens.

"Why do you keep them separated?" Katy asked.

"Mostly because the two dolphins in the smaller pen, Sonny and Cher, have been together all their lives while the others are relative newcomers."

Katy focused on the wooden rail that rose a yard over the lagoon surface, attached to the fence that stretched to the sea floor. "Can't they just jump over that fence?"

"They could, but they don't. It's not natural for dolphins to jump over anything solid that could hurt them if they landed on it. Totally against their nature."

Mike led Katy across the shoreline to the platform closest to shore, where a session was underway in the larger pen. A therapist handed a rubber ball to a boy who tossed it awkwardly into the water so one of the dolphins could swim out to retrieve the ball with her nose.

"Come swim with the dolphins," Katy droned. "I've seen the ads on TV."

"Not for Dolphin Human Therapy you haven't."

"You can call it whatever you want, but the only reason that dolphin fetched that ball is because the guy with the whistle told him to and then fed him when he brought it back."

"That dolphin's a she. And what'd you expect? What we do here isn't magic. We use the dolphins as positive reinforcement, motivation. The attention of the kids we work with, their ability to process information, is increased because of the interaction with the dolphins."

"Sure." Katy rolled her eyes. "Whatever you say."

Mike pointed to the near platform. "That boy's name is Hans. He's over here from Germany."

"What's wrong with him?"

"A bicycle accident three years ago. He suffered a brain injury after he was hit by a train." Katy looked bored. "Stopped speaking, stopped responding to any stimuli. Just stared at the wall all day. No reaction to anything, until he came to Dolphin Key. This is his third week here, and his progress has been unbelievable." Mike pointed toward the pen. "You see what he's doing?"

Katy looked at the boy, who was stroking the side of the dolphin. "Petting it."

"Why?"

"I don't know; maybe he wants to put a leash on the thing, take it for a walk."

"Try again."

Katy turned back toward Mike. "Look, you want to cut me loose, fine. You want to keep me around so you can feel you've done your civic duty, that's fine too. I don't even have to show up. Just sign my reports and you can go to bed with a clear conscience."

Mike's expression remained unchanged. "One more time: Why is the boy petting the dolphin?"

Katy rolled her eyes again. "To reward it for bringing the ball back."

"And the dolphin is rewarding him by *letting* Hans pet her. That provides the motivation he needs to complete the task, a task he couldn't complete last week."

Katy watched Hans toss the ball and the dolphin return it again.

"In a few minutes his therapist will move on to a bigger ball," Mike Fontana said. "Make the boy use both hands to throw it. Then they'll go for a swim and Hans will hold onto the dolphin by himself."

"Big deal."

"It is for him. Hans thinks about doing something, the simplest task, and he hasn't been able to do it since the accident, especially with his right hand, which is partially paralyzed. He gets around the dolphins; he's only thinking about playing with them and the task becomes easier. For over two years, before he came here, that boy lived totally within himself. Every thought, every action, was turned inward, no response to outside stimuli. That's what the dolphin is giving that boy. That's what's lifting Hans out of his shell."

"Maybe they should have just put him on drugs."

"Drugs didn't work; nothing did, until his parents brought

him here. Dolphin Human Therapy brought Hans back into the world."

Katy chuckled. "Maybe he was better off before."

"Why don't you ask him? You can now; you couldn't six months ago. You notice his right hand?"

Katy looked at the boy holding the ball between both his hands. "He's using it."

"That's right."

"One of your regular miracles?"

"Sometimes," Mike said, "we get lucky."

CHAPTER NINE

Mike led Katy Grant around to the southern side of the complex, just beyond the largest of the three lime-colored buildings he and Joe had turned into their home. They passed by an inner pen that was an extension of Sonny and Cher's half of the lagoon, and approached the seawater rehabilitation pool where the dolphin Mike had rescued yesterday at Crandon Park Beach had been placed.

"That boy must be your son," Katy said, noticing Joe carefully guiding the dolphin around the pool.

"How'd you know?" Mike asked her.

"The resemblance is pretty striking."

"Poor kid."

"That dolphin sick or something?"

"I wish I could tell you. So far we've had marine biologists from the Miami Seaquarium and experts from the Rosenstiel School of Oceanographic Studies down, and none of them can tell us for sure. But they put him on antibiotics and that seems to be working. Best guess right now is that he's got a liver disorder. We've also detected a problem with his vision. That's enough to keep us from returning him to the wild, which is the plan if a dolphin gets well enough."

Katy tried not to appear interested, but she couldn't take

her eyes off the activity in the pool. "So what's your son doing?" she asked nonchalantly.

"Keeping the dolphin moving so he can get his strength back. Making sure he gets enough air and coaxing food into him, now that the antibiotics have kicked in. The first day, there were three of us in the water with him to keep the dolphin from banging into the walls. They're not used to swimming in confined spaces."

"He gonna make it?"

"Too early to tell. The great majority don't, but most don't even make it even this far."

Katy watched Joe and the dolphin in what looked like a waterborne dance. "What happens when your kid leaves?"

"Someone else takes his place. The whole staff's been taking turns, along with a stable of volunteers. Twenty-four hours a day at first."

"I've never been much for volunteering."

"Never too late to start. How are you in the water?"

"They filled my apartment's pool in with cement," Katy said, thinking of the ugly slab her window overlooked.

"Don't worry," Mike said, "you'll be in the shallow end. Keep your head above water."

"That'll be a nice change."

Katy changed into a bathing suit Mike found for her to wear and joined Mike in the rehabilitation pool.

"You've got to develop trust with the animal," Mike explained as he guided the dolphin gently along. "That's first and foremost. Show him that you care and he can rely on you, no matter how much he's been through."

"This is what I'm going to be doing here?"

"This is what you're gonna work up to. You start with a broom, a mop, and a hose."

"Sounds a lot like jail to me."

"Except jail's the place where you look at things through bars instead of a scuba mask," Mike said, supporting the dolphin with one hand beneath its head and the other beneath its stomach.

"How'd all this get started?" Katy asked, trailing him around the small pool. "You a marine biologist or something?"

Mike shook his head. "I never even graduated college."

"So where'd you learn about dolphins?"

"I guess you'd call it on-the-job training."

"How about brain injuries, stuff like that?"

"I've been taking night school courses in clinical psychology for a couple years."

Katy snickered. "And that makes you an expert?"

"Not even close," Mike said and looked over at his son, Joe, who was sitting on the dock now, facing the main pens, the top of his wetsuit peeled down and toes curled into the greenish surface of the seawater. Mike loved summers because the boy was here with him all day long, instead of just after school and between homework. Suddenly Joe climbed to his feet and waved at Mike as he jaunted off. He watched the boy dash up the ramp toward the building that had been their home for four months now.

Mike's own father had always been too busy saving the Everglades to have much time to spend with him, working double shifts and sometimes sleeping in a small ranger outpost. Mike remembered trying to wait up for him to come home at night anyway. But he had been asleep the night somebody else showed up with the news that his father's airboat had exploded while pursuing alligator poachers.

It was only recently that Mike realized he had chosen to chase the bottle instead of poachers. And, just like the ones his father had been chasing the night he died, the bottle had gotten the better of him. Mike always thought his father was the toughest guy in the world, had taken to chasing that image prior to the bottle. He signed up for Vietnam to be a hero and came back a drunk after finding he didn't know his father well enough to be like him. Mike had to be himself instead, and he honestly didn't know how.

"Take a couple courses and you're ready to start making the big bucks," Katy resumed, nodding. "Maybe you got a good thing going here, except"—she gazed around her—"this place must've set you back a ways."

"The lease costs me a buck a year, and Gus supplied the two dolphins and enough money to get us started."

"Gus?"

"Probably the best dolphin trainer in the world. He brought his own people in so we'd have a staff. That's him over there."

Katy shaded her eyes to gaze down the dock. "The guy scaring those birds away with his hat?"

"He doesn't like birds, but he loves dolphins. Now, put your hands under this dolphin, near mine," Mike told her.

"If I'm going to be cleaning shit all day, why do I have to do this?"

"Because it's their shit you're going to be cleaning, so to speak. I'd like you to understand that."

Mike eased his hands over hers, positioning them on the proper parts of the dolphin's frame.

"He doesn't feel very heavy at all."

"Because he's swimming on his own now. We're just steering, there in case he needs us."

"Twenty-four hours a day?"

"Not after today."

"Like this?" Katy asked and felt the dolphin squirm a little in her grasp."

"Keep him steady, that's it," Mike cautioned. "Let him get used to your touch. . . . Much better. . . . If things go well, pretty soon we'll introduce him to the others and make him a part of the therapy program."

"Why wait?"

"We've got to make sure Sunset Sam is free of any diseases that he could spread to the other dolphins."

"Sunset Sam?"

"After Sammy Davis, Jr., because of his vision. I name all the dolphins here after singers and rock stars: John, Ringo, Paul, and George in the larger pen; Sonny and Cher in the small one. I'm using Sonny and Cher for my language program."

"What, you're teaching them how to talk?"

"More like building a bridge between dolphin language and ours. I'm trying to develop a system of communication between the two species."

Katy snickered. "Might be better off coming up with a system just for ours."

Mike puckered his lips and blew out some breath. "I'm working on that, too."

"You can start by explaining what I'm doing here."

"I already have."

Katy narrowed her eyes and shook her head a little. "Nah. You could have done your civic duty without picking a pain in the ass like me, coach. Lots of better candidates than me in Metro Dade lockup just waiting for a break."

Mike took a hard swallow that left his expression stiff. "Sure. But only one of them is my daughter."

CHAPTER TEN

"My father's dead," Katy muttered, suddenly fighting for breath. But her voice sounded whiny, young. The voice of a little girl who'd hidden in the corner when her father's steps echoed on the stairs. His face remained lost to her memory. The only thing left was a smell of stale sweat mixed with something like the antiseptic her mother used to treat her cuts.

"I used to be," Mike said, his voice barely audible.

Katy felt a tightness in her chest. Her rib cage ached and she suddenly felt slight stabs of pain in her eyebrows and nose where she had fastened her rings through pierced holes that had begun to close up. She pulled her hands out from under the dolphin's flank. She figured the dolphin would just sink to the pool's bottom, hoped it would. But it continued circling the small pool without assistance, stranding them in the middle.

"This is a joke, right? Some kind of point you're trying to make."

"No joke, no point."

Katy tried to speak but could only shake her head. She pressed her fingers into her temples and started to move out of the pool, stumbling in her haste.

Mike beat Katy to the concrete deck that rimmed the pool,

stood directly in front of her. "I'm not going to let you run away."

"Why not? It's what *you* did. You're the expert. I guess we know who I take after, don't we?" Katy's voice was starting to rise, the stiff breeze blowing it back at her, so she could hear it echo faintly. "So just do what you do best and make believe I don't exist."

Mike's face spasmed as if he'd been stung. "I got you out of jail as soon as I heard."

"You ever think of making contact a little earlier, like maybe when my mother died? You remember her, don't you, your wife?"

Mike stood there like a statue, his muscles hardening into stone. "I was drinking a lot then, didn't even know she was dead until . . . after the funeral."

"Lucky for me it didn't take that long for you to figure out I was locked up."

Mike swallowed hard, collected his thoughts again. "The state had placed you somewhere by the time I was sober enough to talk to child welfare. They still weren't very impressed."

"So you gave up."

"I wasn't considered a fit parent by anyone, including myself."

She planted her hands on her hips and glared at him. "This is what, ten years ago? You were already remarried. Joe must have been—"

"A little over two, I think."

"You smack that wife around, too?"

"No, I just didn't come home."

"Guess you didn't learn your lesson."

"Not soon enough, no."

"You ever tell your new wife about me?"

"No."

"I'm sure you had your reasons."

"I was afraid. Of a lot of things."

"You want to know about being afraid?" Katy said, hearing her voice getting loud again. "Try having a cop come to your door to tell you your mother's dead. And there's nobody around and you don't know a soul in the world."

"I wouldn't have been any good for you. I wasn't any good for myself."

"You son of a bitch," Katy hissed and started to storm forward.

Mike grabbed her by the elbows and held her still.

"Let me go!" She was really screaming now, and a few hundred feet away several heads turned in their direction. "Leave me alone, goddamnit!

"I can't do that," Mike said in a very quiet voice.

"Yes, you can. You're good at it."

But he didn't let go. "You walk out of here, it's back to jail. No third option."

Katy yanked her arms from his grasp and held her ground. "Tell you what, let's make it easy for both of us. I walk out of here and take all the bad memories with me, and all you have to do is file the regular reports with probation."

"So you can go back to that street gang?"

"Closest thing to a family I've had in ten years."

Mike shook his head. "No go. Can't do it."

Katy nodded. "So you think you can make up for everything by springing me from jail. Treat me like that brain-damaged kid who can throw a ball now. Sorry, Dad, too late for us to play catch in the backyard. No big deal. You've got a son to enjoy your sober years with."

She started to walk past him and this time Mike didn't stop her. "The deal is, you stay here and work. You walk out, I turn you in flat."

Katy stopped and swung halfway around. "I don't think you'd do that. Matter of fact, I'd bet on it."

"You'd lose."

"Nothing new." Katy turned back to face him. "You'll come around to seeing things my way before very long."

"Will I?"

"I think I'll punch out for the day now. Come back to-morrow with a whole new attitude; see how long it takes before you give up and throw my ass out of here."

Mike swallowed. "Not this time."

"Sure, you're a changed man. What happened, a swim with the dolphins make you see the light?"

"Something like that," Mike said, his gaze going distant. "But it wasn't enough to make me forget those nights I came home drunk. I see myself doing it, not being able to stop."

"My mother remembered too, right up until the end. Still hoped you'd come back, if you can believe that."

"She was a good lady. She deserved better. So do you."

"You get me out of jail, figure I'll let you off the hook."

"I'm just asking for a chance."

"Be careful, Dad, you just might get what you asked for."

Mike stared at Katy storming away, a hostile stranger he didn't recognize, nothing but the lost years and water-spotted concrete between them. He had hoped to put this discussion off until Katy got into the swing of things, found she liked the place at least a little. As with everything else, though, it hadn't gone as planned. And now all the words were out where he couldn't hold them anymore, left to spoil like meat stuck on the grill in the hot sun.

The sun burned the back of his neck, and Mike could feel its rays digging his shoulders. He was trying to convince himself to go after Katy, when he saw Max Hollister standing at the entrance to Dolphin Key.

CHAPTER ELEVEN

Mike's feet scattered bits of gravel and stone as he raced across the parking lot. Hollister had brought some others with him today, a few of whom held professionally made signs that read FREE THE DOLPHINS or CRUELTY HAPPENS HERE. Still more passed out flyers to motorists on Crandon Park Boulevard who slowed down en route to Bill Baggs State Park to see what all the fuss was about. Hollister himself dealt with anyone who actually pulled into Dolphin Key.

He was wearing khaki-colored cargo pants and a matching vest today. Even though the temperatures stretched into the mid-nineties, he had on a long sleeve shirt, too, as if trying to atone for all the damage he'd let the sun do to his skin in the past. His face was the color of driftwood, so dry and leathery it looked as though the slightest expression might crack it. Mike saw it lacked even the slightest sheen of sweat as he approached.

Hollister turned from the passenger side of a car and straightened stiffly. "Before you say a word, Mike, this parking lot remains the property of the state of Florida. I have every right to be here."

"Don't worry, Max, I only came for a flyer."

Hollister leaned back a little, flinching when Mike came

up and yanked one from the top of the pile he was holding. It was folded in thirds, professionally produced in four-color art on glossy paper.

Mike scanned through the pictures of mistreated, abused, and sad-looking animals. Dogs, cats, chimpanzees, even a few rabbits.

"Not a dolphin in the bunch."

"It's a general brochure."

"I'm sure you explain that to the passers-by."

"The point's the very same."

"Is it? Equating Dolphin Human Therapy with animal experimentation?"

Hollister stepped back a little. "You know the funny thing? How much we've got in common, how much we both love these animals."

"We seem to have radically different ways of expressing it, though, don't we?"

"It comes down to exploitation."

"You really think that's what I'm doing here?"

Hollister's stringy hair glimmered in the sun's glow. "What you're doing here is showing that sometimes swimming with dolphins can help humans. And that is going to inevitably lead to the capture of more dolphins in the wild, even though it's illegal. Not everyone with a pool and a parking lot is going to wait for them to wash up on shore to rescue. Tell me you don't agree."

"If you're talking about regulating Dolphin Human Therapy, I see your point."

"Ah, but how many dolphins will have been captured and held captive by the time the regulation begins? How many quacks will open centers like yours, figuring all they have to do is drop a dolphin into a pen and wait for the miracles to start happening? Make a quick buck."

"You think I'm getting rich here?"

Hollister flashed a smile so thin it barely narrowed the furrows in his parchment-colored flesh. "On the contrary, I'm well aware of your financial situation."

Mike felt the blood beginning to boil behind his cheeks. "How about doing some good for Key Biscayne instead of busting my balls, Max? Preservation of the remaining Australian pine trees on the island maybe, or organizing the raccoon population into a union. Even turning the Miami Marine Stadium into a home for all our wayward cats. You'll have a hell of a lot better chance making any of those happen than shutting me down."

Hollister squinted into the sun burning the sky over Mike's shoulder. "We'll see, Mike," he said. "We'll see."

CHAPTER TWELVE

Mike didn't know what to expect from Stephen Hatch in the boy's second day at Dolphin Key. It was difficult to predict with autistic children. Mike had even considered passing Stephen on to one of the more experienced therapists. But he was a scholarship case and Mike liked to handle those by himself whenever possible. Anyway, he had a gut feeling that Stephen was closer to a breakthrough than anyone realized, and he was determined that it would come before the boy returned home.

Mike had learned plenty from the dolphins. Not to rush things for one, that everything unfolded at its own pace. That was how he had come to grips with the years he had spent in and out of a drunken blitz. Much of that time remained a blur, but he remembered enough of it to recognize the kind of man who always lurked just a single drink away. Mike had gone more than six years without that drink now, long enough for his throat to get scratchy and dry at the mere thought of taking a sip. Booze scared him more than anything, the temptation always there no matter how far away he drew.

Mike hadn't gone through AA, couldn't say what any of the Twelve Steps were. He had started drinking out of fear and had kept at it until a greater fear made him stop. The only time the fear seemed gone for good was during therapy sessions with the dolphins. Feeling them inside his head, washing his conscience clean to the point where he could almost forget eighteen years of ruined lives. Until he walked away from the platform and the memories crept back as the sun dried his skin.

But Stephen Hatch's second session started out even worse than the first. He screamed every time Mike reached out to touch him and covered up whenever Mike reached into the milk crate for some props.

"Let's see what Sonny has to say about this," Mike said, nodding at Gus.

Gus raised an open palm into the air, and Sonny began clacking away, the loud clicks emanating from his blowhole, not his mouth, since dolphins have no vocal cords.

"I think he wants to play with you, Stephen," Mike told the boy, "but you don't want to play with him."

Gus turned his palm down and made a cutting motion. In front of the platform, Sonny flicked some water onto Stephen with his nose. The boy tightened himself into a ball at first but then peered out when the dolphin splashed him again.

"We can go in the water with him if you want, Stephen," said Mike, "but first we've got to do our work."

Gus fed Sonny a fish, and the dolphin circled back in front of the platform. Suddenly the boy pushed himself closer to the platform's edge and dropped his limp right hand into the water. Sonny pushed against it with his nose, and Stephen left it there, his face beginning to brighten just a little. As Gus gave Sonny a new signal, the boy lifted his hand in what looked like an utterly foreign motion and patted the top of the dolphin's head.

Suddenly Stephen's eyes flashed to life for a moment. The boy met the knowing gaze of the creature whose wet skin shimmered in the water beneath him, the hot sun catching both of them in its rays. In the next instant the dolphin shifted so the sun caught the water on an angle that bounced glare off the surface.

But through a crease in the glare Mike glimpsed something change in Stephen's dormant expression. The boy's mouth widened while he continued to stroke Sonny's head. Mike caught a brief flash of white before Stephen's mouth closed up again involuntarily.

"Wow," muttered Martha Wallick, who was charting the session.

"Did you see that?" Mike heard Lorraine Hatch say exuberantly on the shoreline.

"He smiled," her husband replied incredulously. "Stephen smiled!"

The Hatches embraced, looking as though they might jump into the water themselves. Mike twisted Stephen's shoulders around so that the boy faced him on the platform again, then snatched a pair of colored squares from the milk crate.

"Show me the red square, Stephen."

Stephen looked down and gestured with his left hand.

"That's right! Very good! Now pick out the blue square."

Stephen's left hand fluttered again.

"Look up first. Look up at my hands and pick out the blue square."

The boy gazed up slightly, just enough for Mike to see his eyes. He kept those eyes forward this time as he extended his right hand outward.

"Very good!" Mike beamed. "Now I want you to take the blue square from my hand," he said, and slowly stretched both squares out toward Stephen.

The boy looked at them, did nothing.

"Take the blue square from my hand."

Mike extended the blue square further and pulled the red one back. Stephen followed the motion with his eyes and plucked the blue square from Mike's palm, letting it fall to the platform.

"Okay, now the red square." And Mike brought that one forward, just as he had brought the first. It took a few seconds, but Stephen took that square from Mike's palm too and dropped it near the first. "Okay," Mike said to Martha Wallick, "we're going to add shape to the mix as well as color."

She made the appropriate notation on her clipboard, as he pulled a blue circle from the milk crate and held it out along with the blue square.

"Now, Stephen, I want you to pick out the circle. Which one is the circle?"

The boy eyed both shapes, then looked down again.

Mike moved the circle and square back into his field of vision. "Pick out the circle for me, Stephen. Pick out the circle and then we'll go in the water with Sonny. We'll go swimming with Sonny."

Head still down, Stephen reached out and tentatively touched the hand in which Mike held the circle.

"Can you pick out the square for me and then we'll go in the water with Sonny?"

The boy hesitated, then touched the circle again before swinging his body around to face Sonny, who had just popped out of the water in front of the platform. He bounced restlessly on his knees and tugged at the strap holding the life belt around his waist.

Mike eased himself into the water and raised his arms directly in front of Stephen. "Do you want me to help you, or do you want to get into the water on your own?"

The boy stretched his hands out and Mike lowered him

into the water. Mike grabbed one of the boy's hands and extended the palm outward as Gus signaled Sonny to make a slow sweep toward them. As the dolphin slid past, Mike maneuvered Stephen's hand so he touched Sonny all along his entire right side.

The dolphin surfaced in front of Gus for a fish, and Stephen began to fidget in Mike's grasp.

"Do you want to get out of the water or stay in, Stephen? Get out or stay in?"

The boy thrashed to free himself and groped for Sonny.

"Okay, I get the idea. What do you say we go for a ride?"

Gus sent Sonny around toward them, and Mike reached out as he passed and grabbed hold of his dorsal fin, holding tight to Stephen with his other hand.

The boy screeched happily, as Sonny zipped them straight out into the lagoon and then circled back to the platform.

"Want to play with Sonny some more? Then say 'more.' " Mike said, enunciating the word carefully and making sure Stephen could see his lips. "Say 'more.' "

The boy twisted away from him toward the platform. Mike lifted Stephen back to the soft rubber mat he'd been sitting on, and the water rolled off his body into the lagoon.

Mike took a seat next to him on the mat, the boy tracing the dolphin's movement's across the pen. "Stephen. Look at me, Stephen."

The boy turned his way after a few seconds.

"Touch the dolphin," Mike said, holding up a wooden flash card with a picture of a dolphin on it.

Stephen looked back toward Sonny.

Mike angled the dolphin flash card in front of him. "Touch the dolphin, Stephen."

Stephen hit the card with his palm, looking impatient.

"Now, touch the dolphin again," Mike instructed, only this time he held the dolphin flash card in one hand and a dog flash card in the other.

The boy touched the dolphin with barely any hesitation at all.

"That was great! I think we should go in the water again. Do you want to go back in the water?"

Stephen started to slide back into the lagoon, but Mike held him at the shoulders. "Can you say 'in'? I want you to try to tell me you want to go *in*," Mike said, exaggerating the final word. " 'In.' Come on, 'in.' "

Stephen swung away from him, frustrated, and tried to push himself past Mike into the water.

"Okay, kid, just let me go first," Mike said, and slid in ahead of him.

CHAPTER THIRTEEN

Mike found Katy Grant sitting at the head of the docks when he finished skimming the pens the next morning, a cigarette dangling from between her lips.

"I wasn't sure you'd be coming back," he said, sounding a little relieved.

Katy lifted the sunglasses from the bridge of her nose. "Like I told you yesterday, I've got my reasons."

"Did I forget to tell you there's no smoking allowed here?"

Katy laid the narrow sunglasses back over her eyes. "Worried the dolphins will eat the butts?" She emptied a thick lungful of smoke from her mouth.

"We get some people who don't appreciate the smoke."

"Just have the dolphins take care of them." She took a deep drag off her cigarette, then rested her arm on her knee and let the butt dangle there.

Mike stooped and snatched it from her hand, crushing it beneath his sneaker. Without missing a beat, Katy fished a pack of Marlboros from the pocket of her jeans, but left the box closed.

"I'm confused about something," Mike said.

"It happens."

"What I don't get is why you want to go back to jail so badly."

"Did I say that? I'm here to work, play with the good guys for a while. Come on, you, me and Joe—all that family crap. The Waltons of Key Biscayne. Just tell me what you want me to do."

"Yesterday I told you I wanted you here early enough to put out the garbage for the truck. Don't worry, I took care of it."

"I look worried to you?"

"The weekly fish delivery came, too. It needs to be put in the freezer."

Katy climbed angrily to her feet. "How much do these damn things eat?"

"Between fifteen and twenty-five pounds a day, unless the fish spoils."

"Whatever you say, coach," she said and started to walk past him.

Katy had jammed the wooden crates packed with over five hundred pounds of iced herring, squid, mackerel, sardines, and capelin into the freezers without unpacking them. Mike had to crack the wood with a hammer to get the fish out, then invest another twenty minutes prying the crates free.

Covered in slime and sweat, he had emerged from the shed housing the freezers into the searing heat that roasted the air. His hands were splintered and scraped raw, and he had a swollen thumb from a misstrike with the hammer.

Later that afternoon, though, Mike was surprised to find Katy Grant washing down the docks, just as she was supposed to. The front pocket of her shirt held the folded-up page Mike had given her mapping out her daily schedule. The bulge of the Marlboro cigarette box remained evident in her jeans.

"Right on time," Mike complimented.

Katy dumped some suds from the bucket onto the wood. "Actually I'm a day late; I was supposed to do this yesterday. I can see why your friend Gus doesn't like the birds; they leave turds everywhere. Anyway, I figured I'd at least get something done before you sent me back to the county lockup."

"Pretty sure that's what I'm going to do, aren't you?"

"I know you want to."

Mike shook his head. "Sorry to disappoint you. You're staying."

"Why?"

"Because you want to go and I want to throw you out. Too easy for both of us."

"And you're the kind of man who wants to make things hard."

Katy turned and Mike saw the red banshee tattoo of the Dade Flood etched down her bicep just below her rolled-up sleeve.

"They must have gotten you drunk before you got that," he said.

"You should know."

CHAPTER FOURTEEN

The next morning, Mike saw Katy Grant's beat-up Volkswagen Golf as soon as he stepped out of the building where he and Joe were living. He again felt relieved she was here—until he checked on the trash deposit area.

Katy had taken out the trash as ordered all right, taken it out and spilled every bit of it onto the pavement in a formless heap.

He could smell yesterday's leftover thawed-out fish rotting in the early morning sun, most of them lying on the pavement as if they had swum out of the pile. The soda cans, juice containers, fast-food wrappers, and slop swiped off the docks formed the bulk of the pile that must have easily filled four double-thick bags.

"What happened?" Joe asked, right behind him.

Mike looked at his son. "Coyotes."

"More like Katy."

"I warned you this wasn't going to be easy."

"I think I've got an idea."

"Well," Mike told his son, "let's get a couple shovels, and you can tell me all about it."

*   *   *

"You could use a shower," Katy said as Mike began his daily skimming chores. He and Joe had finished rebagging the garbage just in time for the garbage truck to haul it away.

"Know what I'm thinking?"

"That you're going to call probation right now," Katy snapped back, standing there like a person who was already gone.

"Get you tossed back into jail. Give up on you."

"Yeah."

"No. I did that once. I'm not going to do it again."

Katy could only shake her head. "When you going to learn, boss?"

"You enjoy hating me, don't you?"

"I figure I got it coming to me."

"Then you've got something else coming, too, and it's standing right in front of you: me. Keep hating long enough and I'm what you're going to turn out to be. The lost hours and days, even years—they gnaw at you, turn you into somebody no one else likes any more than you like yourself. I let you go and the hate won't let up. You'll be stuck with it for life."

"I'm already stuck."

"So why'd you bother coming back this morning?"

"I had some business to attend to."

"I won't make it easy for you. You want to go, go. But that's going to be your decision too, not mine." Mike gave her a long look. "Tell you one thing. It took a lot more work emptying those bags like you did than it would have just piling them up. That proves you're not lazy. I hope you brought a change of clothes."

"Huh?"

"Give the ones you're wearing a whiff. All that hard work you did must have left something behind."

Katy craned her neck and sucked in the aroma from her shirt. She wrinkled her nose at the stink, sniffed her hands, and then wiped them off on her jeans.

"Wouldn't do that if I were you; the jeans are probably worse. You really should have dressed for the occasion." Mike drew the skimmer from the pen and started up the dock toward his house. "I think I'll take that shower now," he said as he passed her.

Katy drove back to Dolphin Key late that night, running the toll at the entrance to Key Biscayne off the causeway just for the fun of it. She'd always loved the night; the later and darker, the better. The dark was a place to hide when the heavy footsteps pounded up the stairs in her oldest memories. People couldn't find you in the dark, whether it be the closet, the garden, or under the bed.

Later, in her years with the Dade Flood, the dark became a place where she could make things happen. Own the world and have her way with it after everyone else had retreated. Things happened and nobody knew how or why exactly. Cops would trace her and the other Flood members with their bright spotlights. But chunks of the darkness remained, there for the taking.

This was a moonless night, which made it all the better. Katy walked around the far dock enclosing the larger of the two dolphin pens and found the gate that shut the lagoon off from the ocean. It was locked with a simple Master, an easy job she performed with a pick left over from her days with the

Dade Flood. The lock popped open after a few seconds and she yanked it off and dropped it into the water. Then, using both hands, she pushed the gate open.

"Come on, boys," she called softly. Katy couldn't see the dolphins, but she knew somehow that they were watching and listening to her from inside the pen from which she was liberating them. Ungrateful bastards. "I'm setting you free. Time to kiss Dolphin Key and Mike Fontana good-bye. Come on, the door's open. . . ."

The night currents caught the fence and pushed it further open, widening the route into a calm and inviting darkness as the dolphins appeared.

CHAPTER FIFTEEN

Katy couldn't wait to get back to Dolphin Key the next morning, wanted to be there when Mike Fontana awoke to find his world royally screwed. She imagined patients arriving for sessions with dolphins that were no longer around. At least four of them roaming the open seas by now, tossing Mike the flipper while they swam as far from Key Biscayne as possible.

But she arrived to find Mike skimming the top of the pen as he always did while the dolphins he called the Beatles looked on.

"Funny thing," he said, "they got the gate open last night. Guess they needed a swim."

Katy looked from Mike to the dolphins and back again, her stomach tightening.

"Can't blame them, I guess," Mike continued. "We used to let them swim in the open waters every day."

"Outside the pen?"

Mike nodded. "It's called gate training. But a few years ago the federal government passed a law requiring us to keep them penned at all times." As Katy watched, he moved to the gate and fastened a brand-new lock into place. "I guess they just got lucky last night," he said, looking back at her.

Mike reeled the skimmer in, emptying the contents of the

net into a plastic pail. He took the pail in one hand, the skimmer in the other, and started to walk off, stopping before he got very far.

"Oh, I almost forgot," Mike said, and laid the pail down so he could fish Katy's lock pick from the pocket of his shorts. "Found this out on the dock. I thought it might belong to you."

Katy Grant's third day at Dolphin Key ended just as the first two had: mopping down the docks, clearing away anything the day had washed up and left behind. It was almost dusk and no one else was around, the rest of the staff having driven off to a meeting at the Miami Seaquarium and Mike at one of his continuing-education classes. As far as she knew, that meant she was alone with the dolphins. Instinctively, Katy saw this as an opportunity—for what, she wasn't yet sure.

The Beatles swam away at her approach to their pen.

"Where you going, fishies?" she called softly to them. She moved from the dock down onto the nearest floating dock and knelt over the surface. "I gave you the chance to blow this place last night, and you're still here. You boys really ought to get a life. How 'bout I fix you a snack? Some rat poison sprinkled on your daily flounder maybe."

"I don't think they're listening."

Katy nearly jumped out of her skin. She turned to find Joe just behind her.

"It's okay. They don't bite."

"Stay back: I do."

Joe squeezed his features together, sizing her up. "Yeah. My father told me."

"Got yourself a sister, bro." Katy said that expecting to feel something, but she didn't. "What do you think?"

"I haven't decided yet."

"Right. We got some lost time to make up. Tell you what, I'll call some of my old pals in the Flood and we'll make a dry run up South Beach or through the Grove."

Joe's expression loosened a little. "Dry run?"

"A cruise with empty guns hanging out the window. Scare the richies shitless. Make 'em piss in their banana daiquiris."

"How'd you get in the Flood?" Joe asked, his head cocked a little to the side like he was seeing her differently, hearing a new voice.

Katy nodded. "Okay, little bro, here's the story. It's five years back. I was fifteen, fourteen maybe, a sophomore in high school. Four girls were up for membership, and they told us only one was going to make it. The final deciding test was to see who could lift the most stuff out of this convenience store in ten minutes. The store was in Fort Lauderdale, couple miles from the airport, and this older man and woman were behind the counters."

Joe sat down and crossed his legs on the platform, gazing up at her attentively.

"It's cool and cloudy, so we're wearing coats that didn't stand out like they would on a day like this. We go in and sweep the aisles, cramming as much as we can into our pockets. You pretend to drop stuff, stoop down to pick it up when you make your grab. Or you just keep your hands low by the hips, so nobody notices you're doing anything at all."

"Did you have a gun?"

"No, it wasn't like that." Then, "Not that time anyway. A good thing too, 'cause I probably would've used it as things turned out. Anyway, the ten minutes are almost up and the others head for the door. I can't even put my hands in my pockets they're so full, but I don't leave because there's still more time and I'm not about to lose. Getting into the Flood was all I cared about. Nothing else mattered, nothing at all. I guess it was the thrill, pushing the limits, but mostly just not giving a shit. You know what that feels like?"

"No."

"Too bad. So finally I walk out and the old lady is sweeping the gum wrappers off the sidewalk. Seventy years old, hunched over, probably destined to work until the day she croaks, and she looks at me and smiles. *Smiles!* Here it is I just ripped her off and she's leaning on her broom to catch her breath. Maybe she said, 'Have a nice day' or something, I don't remember. Stupid bitch."

"Stupid," Joe agreed, nodding excitedly.

"I got halfway to my friends, who were already crowded into our van parked across the street, when the old man from inside the store came running out. He's screaming in some gook language, holding a baseball bat in both hands. I started across the street again, but the van screeched away before I got there. When I turned around, the old fart swings the bat at me. He was so frigging weak, I just snatched it right out of his hands, thinking about hitting him with it, when his wife starts whacking me with her broom.

"So I'm dodging the blows, and the whole time the stuff I lifted is spilling out of my pockets, and all I can think is how much these old gooks screwed up my day. Anyway, I marched back into the store with the old gooks tripping over themselves to chase me and started smashing things up with the bat. Spilling things over too, racks of bread, a Drake's pastry stand. I remember the doughnuts rolling across the floor, leaving trails of sugar behind. I was still tipping shit when the police got there and tried to slap handcuffs on me. I think I kicked one of them and then one of them whacked me and I don't remember much after that."

"Did it hurt?"

"Like a bastard."

"You go to jail?"

"I got probabation on the condition I make full restitution. The day I dropped off my first payment, I went back to the store and threw a rock through a window."

"But I guess you got in," Joe said.

"To the Flood? Abso-friggin'-lutely. Unanimous vote, even though they couldn't count all the stuff I'd stolen."

"Have a good time?"

"Mostly," Katy said, her voice drifting a little. "It's been nine months since the court told me I'd do time if I got caught associating with them, but here I am anyway, so maybe I shouldn't have listened." She lowered her voice. "Truth is, they wouldn't take me back now anyway."

Joe stood up. "Why not?"

"None of your business, little bro."

The boy looked beyond her toward the dolphins that had sneaked up toward the edge of the platform. "I'll let you swim with them if you tell me," he said, kicking the sandals from his feet and joining her on the platform.

"With the dolphins?"

"Come on, I know you want to."

"They're looking at me funny, from the side."

"That's because they can't see straight ahead. Hey, you're not scared, are you?"

"Might piss your father off."

Joe hesitated, then cracked a slight grin. "He's your father, too."

"I'm beginning to think we've got some blood between us after all, bro."

CHAPTER SIXTEEN

Joe clicked the water to get the dolphins' attention.

"What are you doing?"

"Introducing you."

"What if they don't want to meet me?"

"If they see you with me, they'll like you. That's the way they are."

True to Joe's word, the dolphins swam gracefully straight for him and popped their heads out of the water.

"See?" Joe said. "They like you. They're inviting you in."

Katy looked at the boy. "Will you come with me?"

He shook his head. "It's better alone the first time."

"With all four?"

"Sure."

"You're sure I won't scare them?"

"Worst thing that happens is they ignore you. That happens sometimes."

In spite of herself, Katy turned back to the water. The dolphins had swum away again, the introductions complete. "So I just drop in . . ."

"That's right."

"They're watching me."

"They've seen you around. Wondered why it took you this long to come over probably."

"Okay, here goes." Katy dropped into the water stiffly and grabbed the side of the platform with her hands.

"A couple things you need to know," Joe said, leaning over her. "Don't reach out to touch them right away; let the dolphins make the first move. Swim with your hands by your sides, and don't swim directly at or behind them—they sometimes see that as hostile."

Katy worked herself out deep enough to tread water. "Great."

"Don't worry. They like women second best after children. It's men they sometimes have a problem with, but not very often. Now swim out a little more."

The dolphins were still watching her, in between glances at each other as their heads bobbed about the surface.

"They're laughing at me."

"Just another human fool who can't swim very well, that's all."

"Do they think there's something wrong with me?"

"Depends if there is or not," Joe said, suppressing a laugh.

Katy dropped beneath the surface and swam slowly toward the dolphins. The water was murky and she couldn't see them too clearly. But suddenly she heard something, like a rapid bubbling under the water. Then a streak of silver and white flashed by directly below. Before she could react, two more of the dolphins surged by on either side of her. They looked massive, and Katy realized seeing them from a safe distance, with only their heads above water, had provided her a comfortable illusion. But close-up, within their domain, she remembered the biggest one was nine feet long and weighed seven hundred pounds.

Katy swam slowly on, trying not to appear intimidated. She continued away from the dock toward the middle of the pen, deeper into the dolphins' world. They swam past her again, crisscrossing each other's wakes and enclosing her in a vortex of bubbles. More approaches followed, with each bringing them closer to her until a collision, at least a bump, seemed inevitable. But always the dolphins veered away at the last second.

They're testing me. See what I'll do.

Up to the challenge, Katy simply paddled on, kicking lightly. The dolphins slowed. One of them came up alongside and made eye contact with her, holding it.

Katy felt a wave of exultation surge through her. She knew what it was like staring into the eyes of a person as well as an animal, and this was no animal. Like everyone else, she had always assumed dolphins were smart because that's what everyone said. Until that lingering moment, though, she hadn't realized *how* smart.

She sucked in some breath and dove deeper, trying to follow the dolphins down. Then, all at once, she felt a burst of static inside her brain, like the feeling of holding a knife against the inside of a toaster. She heard a sound in her head that had come in via some route other than her ears and shuddered, not with fear or panic but euphoria.

As if to acknowledge the contact they had achieved, one of the dolphins opened its mouth and seemed to blow out some water. At that point Katy realized the other dolphins were watching her as well, pinging her the way submarines do with their sonar. She stopped swimming and just let herself relax in the seawater. In that instant she felt at peace, incredibly at ease with herself, as if the dolphins had flushed all the bad feelings, all the bad times, out of her.

The one she had made eye contact with first swam closer and nudged her gently in the shoulder with its nose, the moment full of power and grace. Katy didn't move, just lay suspended in the water until the dolphin swam up alongside her and she couldn't resist reaching out and touching its skin. Her hand continued down its sleek flank as it stretched slowly past. She heard it make a cackling noise but felt certain, somehow, the sound wasn't aimed at her. Had the dolphin passed on its approval of her to the others? Or was it saying, don't bother, boys, this one's a loser?

She found herself unaccountably wanting to please these creatures, be accepted by them, more than she had wanted anything in a very long time. The pinging stopped and her head emptied of the invisible sound.

Katy watched as the dolphins glided away from her. She was tempted to swim after them, reluctant to let go of the moment they had given her. She wanted them inside her head again, wanted to feel that warm rush of security they spread like a blanket on a cold night. But they were gone and she headed back toward the dock.

"They zapped me," she said to Joe, leaning her upper body atop the old wood. "Like I had a funny bone in my head and they hit it."

"It's called echolocation."

Katy realized she felt incredibly relaxed, every part of her body supple and loose. "What's it mean?"

"Nobody knows for sure. There are lots of theories, from some sort of telepathy to a kind of psychic CAT scan. That's the way cancer patients describe it anyway."

"Cancer patients come here?"

"A few."

"Does it help?"

Joe looked away from her back toward the dolphins. "Sometimes."

"Do you think they liked me?"

Joe slapped her playfully and ran off. "Not if they're smart."

That night Mike and Joe went for walk on the strip of beach that rimmed the Key Biscayne shore. Mike thought of his father as they passed developments with names like the Grand Bay and the Ocean Beach, wondered what his father would think about all these high-rise condominiums sprouting up to consume the island like out-of-control weeds.

"How'd she do?" Mike asked his son.

"Pretty good. Just about like I told you she would."

"She never suspected?"

"Not a thing."

Mike grabbed the boy's shoulder and drew him in. "We make a pretty good team, know that?"

TWO

CHAPTER SEVENTEEN

"I want to work with the dolphins," Katy told Mike in his office the next morning.

He looked up from the paperwork scattered across his desk. "You are."

"I'm cleaning docks and icing down fish."

Mike noticed Katy had taken out her eyebrow and nose rings. "Still got that tool of yours I found on the dock the other day?"

"No."

"I guess it outlived its usefulness."

Katy felt something tingle in the back of her neck. She hadn't been able to get the dolphins out of her head after her swim with them the previous night. Every time she had started to fall asleep, the feeling of sharing the water with the dolphins returned, and she woke up missing the strange peace and contentment that they had brought her. They had let her into their world, welcomed her even, and she'd been able to think of nothing else since.

"I made a mistake," she said softly.

"That's right, you did."

"I was angry. I figure I had that coming to me."

"You did. But now you're asking me to trust you."

"I know."

"That's asking a lot."

Katy watched him turn away, busy with other thoughts. "Would it help if I said I was sorry?"

Mike looked back at her. "I'll bet you don't say that too often."

"No."

"Must have been hard."

"You bet. Just give me a chance. That's all I'm asking."

Mike looked like he was thinking about it. "You'll need to start taking some courses at the college. Just one or two for starters at night."

Katy nodded. "I can handle that."

"You have a high school diploma?"

"GED."

"Good enough. I'll make some calls, put the wheels in motion. If you're up to it, I'll pay the whole ride."

"When do I start?"

"School?"

"Here. With the dolphins."

Mike rubbed his chin. "I guess we could call you an intern."

"Means I have to wear one of those dorky Dolphin Key T-shirts, right?"

"Identifies you as part of the staff."

"One big happy family . . ."

"Do you have a problem with that?"

Katy held her eyes open. "Just not used to it, that's all."

Mike hesitated, looked down briefly at his desk. "Would you like to know what an intern does?"

"I've been watching."

Mike held up a trio of manila folders. "It starts with these forms. First thing we do with a client is take a history and make a careful list of goals and objectives. For the clients you're assigned to, it's your job to know that history along with those goals and objectives backwards and forwards. Got it?"

Katy was ready to fire off something clever but managed to hold her tongue and just nod instead.

"Now the main job of an intern is to keep exact documentation of each of your clients' progress. That means detailed descriptions of each interaction with the dolphins; the child's response and the animal's response. You do that immediately after each session on another form. I'll pull out some samples for you to go over."

Katy felt herself pulling back. "I've never been much good at that sort of stuff."

"Neither was I when I started," Mike said, continuing before Katy had a chance to respond. "Since all our clients have special needs, lots of times we generate a form just for them. If their problem is speech, we chart every single word and sequence of words they utter. If they don't speak at all, we chart every sound they make. That's what you'll be doing as the session's going on and after it's finished, so I can review all the results after the day's over and present them at the regular staff meeting."

Katy took the folders Mike extended toward her, awed by their bulk. "You learn all that at night school?"

"I've learned to listen to people who know a lot more than I do. Now find a quiet place and go over those forms," Mike said finally. "Familiarize yourself with the kind of things we do here, and pay special attention to the file on a seven-year-old girl with Williams syndrome named Jilly Previn."

"Why?"

"Because we've got a session with her this afternoon at one o'clock. Don't be late."

Mike did his best to hide his smile until Katy was out the door. She nearly bumped into Jacardi Benoit on the way. The look on the big Haitian's face was enough to tear Mike's smile away even before he spoke. He had the taut grimace of a man fighting back pain.

"I saw your little one on the road this morning, mombo," he said, his face glistening with sweat in spite of the morning breeze that washed the clean scents of the sea and the flowering tropical plants through the open office window. "Just a few minutes ago on my way to the college."

Mike kept listening, knots tightening inside him.

"I pull over and ask him what he's doing, tell him to get in the car and I'll take him wherever he wants to go." Jacardi's eyes sought out Mike's. "He said he's going nowhere. That's the problem, he says. I see he's been crying and I know there's something wrong and I ask him if his father knows where he is. Then he gets very stiff and walks away from me, mombo. I ask him where he's going and he won't say, won't even turn. So I come straight here because I'm sure it's not right, whatever's going on."

Mike started for the door, sliding past Jacardi.

"You not gonna ask me where I saw the little one, mombo?"

Mike turned, but only briefly. "No need; I know where he's going."

The William Powell Bridge linked Key Biscayne to mainland Florida along the Rickenbacker Causeway. But before its construction in the eighties, another unnamed bridge had served that task. This one was of the draw variety and had to be opened anytime a ship with a mast taller than forty feet passed through. Massive traffic jams began to result once Key Biscayne's population boomed. So Miami officials passed a bond issue enabling them to slice away the old bridge's much cursed center span and build the William Powell well above it.

The arms of the older span still remained intact, jutting out hopelessly toward each other, the space between them forever breached. The old, rusting structures had become like twin piers for fishermen and teenagers alike. The teenagers came looking for a place to hang out, seldom before dark, while the fishermen were almost always gone before they arrived.

Mike found Joe leaning against the old bridge's safety rail. His feet were wedged beneath it, toes curled over the lip. He was staring straight ahead, face dappled by thin patches of sunlight sneaking through the shadows. He didn't turn when Mike came up and stood next to him.

"The cancer," Joe said, wiping his nose. "I think it's back."

CHAPTER EIGHTEEN

"I found a lump," Joe said flatly, turning his neck.

Mike reached out and felt Joe's neck. The boy's flesh was hot and damp to the touch. The swollen gland felt like a marble fighting its way through the skin.

"It could be an infection," Mike grasped, in search of another explanation. "A virus or something."

"It's not," Joe said, and sat down so his jean shorts squished a little against the deck's wet surface.

"It went away the last time. Seven months ago, just before we moved to Dolphin Key. Remember?"

Joe looped his hands through the railing before him like the bars of a cell. "I don't know. Maybe."

Mike tried not to look as scared as he felt. He'd never fully trusted all the various diagnostic devices and tests, fearing the bad cells were just hiding, camouflaged to the immune system and invisible to the best machines money could buy.

He'd been sober for more than a year when Joe was first diagnosed with Hodgkin's disease at the age of eight. Mike had quit drinking the day his second wife, Joe's mother, walked out on both of them. He remembered that clearly because the news from the doctor hit him the same way things did when he was drunk: the words not quite getting through, stuck in the netherworld his brain had forged for itself out of bourbon and scotch. He thought he had heard wrong, asked the doctor to repeat himself.

It was first stage, though, maybe a 95 percent chance for a complete recovery. The chemo and radiation had been tough, but not as tough as news of the recurrence Joe suffered a year later. More chemo, lots of it, getting him ready for a bone marrow transplant the doctors insisted provided the best, perhaps only, chance for a remission. Mike had been working for the city of Miami in those days, and the health plan, thankfully, covered everything.

It was after the bone marrow transplant, almost three years ago now, that Mike had read about the work being done by Dr. David Nathanson down in Key Largo. One of Nathanson's therapists had served in the 101st in Vietnam, and Mike worked a free series of sessions out of him after reading about the often seemingly miraculous effects of Dolphin Human Therapy. Joe had just gotten out of the hospital, so his hair hadn't started to grow back yet, and a pair of dolphins kept nuzzling his bald head.

Even though he hadn't joined his son in the water, even though the closest he got to the dolphins was the platform, Mike felt the tingle. And on that day he decided he wanted to open a facility just like Nathanson's. He didn't know anything about dolphin training or clinical psychology, but he wasn't going to let either of those factors stop him. He tracked down a retired trainer named Gus Anton over the Internet and drove down unannounced to meet him in Marathon. He found Gus there with a pellet gun, scaring birds away from a pen housing his two dolphins and swearing up a storm in German. As luck would have it, Gus had been getting the urge to get back to work, although he told Mike the whole notion was crazy. But

Mike told him he had a facility already picked out and he hadn't seen a bird around the area yet.

The lies worked.

Of course, the next challenge was finding a site, but the costs proved astronomical the few occasions Mike had been able to locate one. The problem was he needed deep water close to shore, and digging out anything other than silt was prohibited these days for environmental reasons. That left as Mike's only options an existing marine facility or a marina, the price for either stretching into the millions. He was about to tell Gus Anton to forget it when he happened upon the ruined marina in Bill Baggs State Park.

Giving Mike a long-term lease at a dollar per year allowed the marina's owner to take depreciation on the property after he had already collected the insurance for the damage wrought by Hurricane Andrew. Gus Anton winced when he saw the facility's decrepit condition, then offered to lend Mike the money he needed to bring it up to standard. And while Mike was busy at Home Depot, Gus was contacting four of the trainers who used to work under him to offer them all jobs.

Gus owned Sonny and Cher himself, which gave them a start. But the prohibitive cost of captive dolphins, up to $300,000 each, seemed to rule out getting any others. Again not about to be denied, Mike suggested linking Dolphin Key with the Rosenstiel School of Oceanographic Studies in the hope of acquiring rescued dolphins instead. After officials there tentatively agreed, Mike began dividing his time between hammer and notebook, learning everything he could about dolphins.

Then he enrolled in his first night school class, taught by Jacardi Benoit at Miami Dade Community College. Like Gus Anton, the big Haitian thought Mike was crazy but still took him under his wing, accelerating his education and squeezing Mike into courses that were already full to help him develop a sense for the kind of patient problems he would be faced with. Jacardi also helped Mike find and select the therapists who would be working alongside Gus's trainers.

Mike was so happy just to have things up and running that he failed to properly consider the mammoth day-to-day expenses involved. If Dolphin Key broke even, that was good enough for him. He never turned down a single child for lack of money, knowing how the parents felt from his own experience.

The truth he had never shared with anyone else, though, was that the dolphins had changed his life as well as Joe's that day at Dave Nathanson's center in Key Largo. They got into his head and showed him life as it could be instead of the way to which he'd resigned himself. They had worked on the twisted scars the past had left inside him to the point where the memories seemed more distant and foreign, the events long out of his control not nearly as important as those still within it. It felt as if the dolphins had washed him clean, swiping away the dark patches so he could see the hope that lay beyond them.

The night after he visited Nathanson's center, he had a dream in which he was certain the dolphins told him his son was going to be all right. To prove it, they played a picture in his head. There was Joe, his color back and his chestnut hair bouncing as he ran along the beach. Pull back a little and there was Mike running alongside him. Tossing a football that turned into a Frisbee.

He had listened to the dolphins then and hadn't stopped listening since. When the last scare came seven months back, he traded their house for a shack so Joe could be near the dolphins day and night. Mike had come to realize these animals lived within the field they created, as if it were a bubble centered on the sea. And if the bubble extended far enough, the boy would be safe.

Looking at his son now on the William Powell Bridge, sniffling and wiping his eyes as he fought back tears, Mike found himself wanting a drink more than at any time since that day a CAT scan had confirmed the bad news five years ago. He could feel the scratchiness in his throat, the dull ache in his head only a chug or two could relieve.

Mike sat down next to Joe on the old bridge and stuck his legs under the lower rail. From this angle, the lump on Joe's neck was barely visible.

Joe looked out over the water toward the gulf. "I thought we had it licked this time."

"We should wait and be sure. We shouldn't jump to any conclusions."

Joe turned and collapsed in Mike's arms. "I don't want to die, Dad! *I don't want to die!*"

CHAPTER NINETEEN

Mike took Joe to breakfast at Jimbo's, a restaurant tucked into a hidden grove on the eastern side of Virginia Key, which adjoined Key Biscayne. Mike had spent a lot of time there in his drinking days, preferring the place to others because they gave him a bottle and left him alone. The isolated shack had never attracted a lot of new customers. Lots of fellow Vietnam War vets had hung out there, whom Mike could identify with a glance, along with bikers and some of the more hard-core locals. The parking lot, as a result, was usually filled with Harleys and pickup trucks.

When he pulled into that lot with Joe by his side today, Mike was struck by how little the place had changed over the past six years. A familiar grouping of picnic tables lay to one side of the building facing the road, shaded the same maple color as Jimbo's itself. The parking lot was mostly empty this time of the morning, and Mike got a thick feeling in the back of his throat as he climbed out of his truck. He may have been coming back to a home that didn't belong to him anymore, but he remembered all too well what it was like to be hurrying toward the door, already tasting the bourbon and longing for its hot swipe down his throat.

That door stuck briefly to the jamb when Mike pushed it

inward and led Joe toward a table on the right. The bar was set, though nobody was drinking. The thickness in Mike's throat settled in a dry throb that left him licking his lips.

"Is that who I think it is?" a woman asked, barging through the swinging doors that led into the kitchen. "Goodness gracious, sakes alive, it's Mike Fontana in the flesh!"

It took Mike a few seconds to recognize Maggie Potts, who had founded Jimbo's with her husband just after he came back from Vietnam. The Jimbo who had given the restaurant its name caught much of the restaurant's fish supply himself and was lost at sea doing just that during a hurricane watch in the late eighties. Neither he nor his boat was ever found, and Mike remembered Maggie being forever convinced that one day he would walk unceremoniously through the restaurant's thick wooden door with a hell of a story to tell. To this day Mike had heard she stubbornly maintained her husband's proud tradition of illegally feeding the manatees that regularly visited the shoreline of Virginia Key in Jimbo's backyard.

Maggie had added some heft to the large frame he embraced when she hugged him tight. Her hair had the look of a perm thwarted by the blistering air of the kitchen, the ends gnarled and shiny with grease and perspiration. But she smelled like wildflowers and her grasp felt warm and good.

"I thought you were dead, Mike."

"Close, Mags. Not quite."

"Off the sauce, though."

"Yeah, and it's the reason why I'm still alive."

"I'll drink to that when I'm alone." Her big wet eyes fell on Joe. "Don't tell me this is your son."

"It appears I don't have to."

"I always figured anything that sprang from your loins

would belong in a pet shop window." She smiled at Joe. "I stand corrected."

A cook popped his head out of the kitchen and called her name.

"I gotta be getting back to work." She gave Mike another hug. "Don't be a stranger anymore."

She returned to the kitchen. Mike and Joe took a table, and a waitress working a wad of gum came over with order pad in hand. "I get you boys some coffee?"

"Please," said Mike, looking at Joe.

"Orange juice," the boy said, and the waitress left to fill their order. "I'm not hungry," he continued when she was gone.

"I never brought you here before. I wanted you to see it."

Joe made a point of looking around. "Okay, I've seen it. Can we go now?"

"You should eat something."

"No. I said I wasn't hungry, didn't I?" The boy looked down at the table and left his eyes there. "That woman a friend of yours?"

"In another lifetime." Mike flipped through the menu. "Pancakes," he said. "I'll bet they're good here."

"You ever have them?"

"This place didn't used to be open for breakfast, unless you happened to be here all night."

Joe rolled his eyes and tugged at the tablecloth. "Can we go home? Please. I'm really not hungry."

"I didn't bring you here just to eat."

"No?"

"I brought you here because this is where I used to come to solve all my problems."

"Nothing on the menu that can solve mine, Dad."

"It was when I was drinking with men like Maggie's husband and a few others I knew from Vietnam."

Joe hedged. "Is that when you started? When you got back from the war, I mean."

"Just about, yeah."

The boy's eyes narrowed in curiosity. " 'Cause of what happened over there, what you saw and stuff?"

"I suppose. I should have gotten help from doctors, I guess, but I was too proud. That wasn't me. I could handle things all by myself. The truth was the only time I felt good was when I was drinking, so I didn't want to stop. It started in the war, because the drinking let us forget where we were. Then I got home and found I didn't like it there either. Only thing the two places had in common was the booze."

"What about Katy?"

"She was born nine months to the day after I got home. I was drunk in the hospital. I told myself I was celebrating. I was always telling myself something."

The boy stiffened, turning sideways as if to get as far from his father's words as possible. "Did you really hit her?"

"Yes, I did, and I'm ashamed of it. But those years weren't about drinking so much as quitting. Drinking was the same thing as quitting, giving up, running away. But when I stopped drinking I swore I'd never run from anything again. You know why I brought you here today?"

"To buy me one?" Joe asked, looking up.

The way the boy said it made Mike feel instantly better. He could feel his muscles relax like rubber bands given back their slack, and he smiled. "No, because I was afraid I might come back here alone. And if that happened, I wouldn't be any better than I was when I kind of made this my home. Because of you I haven't been back in a ton of years. Because of you I got through it. Just like you're going to get through this, whether it's a virus . . . or something else."

Across the table, Joe swallowed hard. The color was back in his face, his eyes aglow with life again.

"I brought you here," Mike continued, "because when we're together I don't need to drink, I don't need anything. That's the way it is."

"But it wasn't enough, was it? That's why you finally found Katy."

"She asked to work with the dolphins this morning, just like we figured."

"What'd you tell her?"

"That I'd give her a chance."

"Think she'll give you one?"

"I hope so."

The boy shrugged. "The dolphins like her."

"That's something."

Joe tightened his expression. "I don't want any doctors. Not right away anyway."

"Your call."

"It could be a virus."

"We'll wait awhile and find out. Say, a couple weeks."

The waitress came with Mike's coffee and Joe's orange juice, whipped out her order pad as soon as she had placed both down. "Now, what else can I get you boys?"

CHAPTER TWENTY

Jilly, the seven-year-old girl with what Mike Fontana had called Williams syndrome, arrived right on schedule at one o'clock. She was accompanied by a stoop-shouldered old man who introduced himself as her grandfather.

"Name's Homer Tiebolt," he greeted.

"Katy Grant."

He looked at her in her staff version Dolphin Key T-shirt. "You new here?"

"Yes."

"I used to be a lawyer. Mess up with my granddaughter and I'll sue you," he said and then winked.

"I'm no stranger to court," Katy said and winked back.

When Mike joined them, he was still looking a bit harried. He had spent much of the morning in his office, Katy popping in only long enough to return the file folders she had been studying through the morning. She focused mostly on Jilly's history, not understanding many of the notations and terminology. She had intended to ask Mike some questions but changed her mind when she saw he clearly had other things on his mind.

That no longer seemed the case once they got Jilly into the kitchen and went about getting the dolphin Paul's bucket of food ready for feeding. Then, shadowed by Homer Tiebolt, who kept an unlit pipe stuffed in the corner of his mouth, they headed back outside and sat down on the platform of the near seawater pen. The hot sun had burned through the morning clouds, a stiff breeze the day's only saving grace. The breeze filled the air with the clean scent of the sea and turned the usually placid cove currents to whitecaps that flirted with the shoreline.

Katy had brought a life belt with her for Jilly and waited for Mike's prompt to ease the little girl into it. He maneuvered Jilly so that she was facing him with Katy seated behind her. Katy watched him remove a pile of large, waterproof flash cards from the milk crate and lay them down on the floating platform next to the bucket of Paul's food.

"Say hello to Paul, Jilly," Mike urged when the dolphin surfaced directly in front of them.

The little girl waved happily at the dolphin. "Hi, Paul," she greeted, her speech slurred as if the words had melted together in her mouth.

"Is there something else you want to ask her?"

Jilly looked at Mike questioningly, then pointed a finger at the steel bucket of food.

"That's right. Now ask her, just like you did last time."

It took the little girl a few moments, but she turned to the dolphin. "You hungry, Paul?"

Gus had Paul nod her head vigorously.

"Okay, Jilly," said Mike, "pick out a fish to feed Paul. A small fish."

Jilly leaned sideways to peer into the bucket. She rubbed her cheek with her hand and then plunged it into the selection they had just washed, feeling carefully about until she came out with a sardine.

"That's perfect, Jilly. Now hold it over the edge."

As she watched Jilly feed the sardine to the dolphin, Katy remembered from her history how such simple reasonings were impossible for the little girl just a few months before.

"That was awesome!" Mike told her, and this time he gave the girl a hug.

Katy stiffened as Mike selected three of the big cards from his pile. She couldn't ever remember him hugging her as a child, not even once. All she remembered was the fear that came when she heard the downstairs door slam and his drunken footsteps clamoring up the staircase. Katy hid in the closet, squeezed amidst the games they never played together.

"Remember this game, Jilly?" Mike asked, as he laid a trio of cards out so they were facing her.

The little girl reached toward the bucket of fish again instead of responding.

"We'll feed Paul again after we play the game," Mike told her. "How do these cards go, Jilly? Put them where they belong."

Jill started to reach for the bucket again, then changed her mind and started studying the cards, sticking a finger in her mouth in much the same way her grandfather held his unlit pipe as he watched from the shoreline.

"Kids like Jilly have tremendous problems with sequencing," Mike explained, looking briefly at Katy. "Putting things in order. This is another of the ways we try to help them."

The three cards Mike had laid before Jilly were of a boy building a fire, lighting the fire, and the fire blazing—in the wrong order. Jilly laid the building card in the proper place, then studied the remaining two. Katy found herself rooting for her to get the next one right, amazed something like this could matter to her today when yesterday she would have laughed at the possibility.

Jilly switched the building card with the blazing card to create the proper sequence.

"Very good!" Mike said, hugging her to him again.

Jilly laughed, then squirmed from his grasp in favor of the food bucket from which she extracted a squid. Mike helped her ease it over the edge of the platform, waiting for Paul to open her mouth. Then he let go and the squid plopped to the water just short of the dolphin's waiting jaws.

"Hungry!" said Jilly.

"Yes, she is," Mike agreed. "Paul's very hungry. What trick should we have her do?"

The little girl lifted a down-turned palm into the air.

"Make her jump? Okay, whatever you say."

And behind her Gus gave Paul an almost identical signal. In the next instant the dolphin soared out of the pen and dove gracefully back in, drawing barely a splash from the surface.

Mike set a new sequence of cards down in front of Jilly. This one featured a young girl playing with dominoes: setting a few up, completing the task, and then finally spilling them over.

"Which one's first, Jilly?" Mike asked.

Jilly finally turned away from the dolphin and picked the card in the center that showed just a few of the dominoes in place.

"Very good. What's next?"

She seemed to puzzle over that briefly before selecting the card with the dominoes spilling over.

"What has to happen before that? What has to happen before you can knock all the dominoes down?"

Jilly's face tightened in concentration and she slapped a finger down on the card portraying the black pieces all neatly lined up.

"That's it! Very good! We're almost ready to go swimming now. Just one more thing to do."

Mike reached behind him and grabbed a trio of plastic rings.

"Rings!" Jilly exclaimed.

"That's right. What color is this one?"

"Throw it!"

She made a motion to grab for the ring, but Mike pulled it back.

"Tell me what color it is first, Jilly. Come on, you know."

"Green!"

"That's right—green. What about this one?"

"Red."

"Not red."

"Blue."

"Very good—blue. And this one?"

"Blue."

"Come on, you know it's not blue. You know what it is. It's your favorite."

"Red!"

"Red—yes. Now you can throw the rings so Paul can go get them for us."

Jilly moved for them again and this time Mike let her have them. She tossed the rings awkwardly out into the pen, and Gus gave Paul the signal to retrieve them. Seconds later the dolphin returned with all three hanging from her nose.

Mike leaned over and took them back, while Jilly applauded happily. "How about we go for a swim with Paul now?"

*   *   *

"This might not look like much," Mike said to Katy, as she cleaned up the platform after the session was over, "but for a child with Williams syndrome to make these kinds of associations is amazing, especially compared to the way Jilly was when she first started in the program."

"What's the trick?"

"There isn't one. Children like Jilly spend their lives focusing on what they can't do. Here we allow them to focus on what they can, allow them to progress in spite of their restrictions. Gives them something to do that no one can. Makes them feel special instead of different."

Katy hardened her gaze. "I know what's it like to be different."

"Not like this."

"You want to talk about being different? Try listening to your friends in school talking about their fathers and all the things they do together. For a while, I made a father up. Used to say how he took me places and bought me ice cream and watched movies with me."

Mike swallowed hard. "Why'd you stop?"

"I grew up. Eight years old, I stopped listening to my friends' stories because I was afraid I might tell them the truth. Then mom died and I had something else to tell them instead."

"I wish I could go back and change things. I would if I could."

"Instead you help little kids like Jilly. It makes you think you're a better man, but they're just strangers you can send home after an hour."

"I know," Mike said. "That's why you're here."

CHAPTER TWENTY-ONE

As soon as the session with Jilly was over, Mike's thoughts returned to Joe and the terrible fear that his cancer had come back. It was strange how he could block everything out when working with a client, the entire world reduced to just the two of them and the dolphin. An hour in which time was frozen.

He knew the process was therapy for him, too. Focusing on what *he* could do, instead of all the lousy things he had done. A cop-out maybe, especially considering the irony that he couldn't help his son and hadn't helped his daughter. But strangers came to him and went away different and better.

Mike told parents that Dolphin Human Therapy was about focusing less on restrictions, about their kids moving forward and overcoming their limitations. But Mike accomplished this by losing himself in their problems, helping them as if intrinsically aware it was as close as he could come to helping himself.

Unless he could reach Katy. At least she genuinely wanted to be here now, thanks to the dolphins, and now it was up to Mike to keep the process going.

He had forgotten who his next session was with until Zachary Haas appeared before him, shuffling down the dock.

"I want to go swimming!" the boy screeched enthusiastically as he bounded forward on his stumps, already wrapped in his life jacket. The afternoon sun had dipped behind a welcome cloud, and the boy squinted up at the sky when it reappeared.

Mike felt himself sliding back into the world he knew best. He helped Zach down onto the platform, where Gus Anton was waiting.

"What do we do now?" the boy asked.

"How much do you really want to swim?"

"A lot!"

Mike fingered his chin dramatically. "You know what might help?"

"What?"

"If we used your prostheses."

The boy looked away. "I hate them."

"Just for swimming. They'll help me teach you."

"No."

"It might be the only way you can swim with George."

The boy shrugged, then nodded. "Okay. I guess so."

Mike accepted the shoulder harness from Katy, who had carried it to the dock. It was a bulky-looking contraption that fastened around the boy's shoulders, with tubular extensions that attached to the stumps of his arms. Zach hated both this and the lower body prosthesis that attached to his hips, thought they were "geeky" and refused to wear them, in spite of the added freedom they would someday provide. To gain more independence, though, he would have get over the fear and reluctance—one of the stated goals on the form his parents had filled out his first day here.

"Now," Mike said as Zach shifted uneasily to get used to the prosthesis, "lie down on the mat on your stomach."

Mike watched the boy maneuver himself into place over the mat that lay across the front of the platform and thought how great it would be if there were some magical prosthesis that could cure cancer. Something he could strap onto Joe that would make his son well.

"What should I do now?" Zach asked, drawing Mike back.

Mike lay down on the platform next to him, trying to push away his own fears. "Arch your back like this and pretend you're a worm. . . . That's it. Good. . . . Now, as you bring your spine forward again, rotate your shoulders out in front of you."

Zach did so and his prosthetic extensions got wedged in the mat. "Oops."

"No," Mike told him, "that was perfect. They won't get stuck when you're in the water. Let's try it again."

Zach squirmed to free his prostheses and repeated the drill. This time he angled the extensions of his stumps so they dragged across the mat instead of digging in.

"Okay," Mike said a few minutes later, "let's try it in the water."

He lowered himself into the warm lagoon first, treading water with one arm while he held the little boy in his other. "I'm going to hold on to you while you do the very same thing you did on the mat."

Zach was tense and unsure at first, but Mike felt him gradually relax and begin to slice his prosthetic arms through the water. Mike held the boy less and less until he was barely supporting him around the stomach, the boy holding the surface on his own, coughing out the occasional water that spilled into his mouth. George kept surging past them, slowing occasionally to watch as if curious.

"Think you're ready to let George see how you're doing?" Mike asked Zach.

"You bet!"

"Then let's show her."

CHAPTER TWENTY-TWO

"Who's the next patient?" Mike asked late the next morning.

Katy consulted her clipboard. "Sarah Beeks."

"Condition?"

"Developmental disability."

"Specifically?"

"She can't speak."

"Can't or won't?"

"Well, she can talk but has a problem forming thoughts into words."

Mike nodded, satisfied. "Much better."

"That's what her form said."

"I know; I filled it out."

"But I don't get it."

"Picture it like this," Mike explained. "Sarah understands everything you say to her. Her intelligence level is basically normal for a six-year-old girl. But something's blocking the transition of thoughts into words. You read her progress charts?"

"You told me to, didn't you?"

"So what do you think we're trying to do for her?"

"Remove whatever's blocking, what'd you call it, this transition."

"Not exactly," Mike told Katy. "We try to teach her how to use her mind to build a new road *around* the block."

"The big guy Jacardi teach you that?"

"We covered it in one of his classes. Come on, let's go to work."

Sarah was waiting for them in the kitchen, already holding a full bucket of fish.

"What's in the bucket, Sarah?" Mike asked her.

The little girl's eyes narrowed and her face tightened. For a moment, her lips moved but no sound emerged. "Fish," she said finally.

"That's right." Mike beamed. "Fish. Now let's go feed them to your friend John."

After they had sat down on the platform, Mike pulled a squid from the bucket. "What's this, Sarah?" he asked as John poked his head over the surface before Gus had even called him.

"Fish!"

"What kind of fish? Can you tell me the fish's name?"

"Squ . . ."

"That's it. Keep trying."

"Squid," Sarah completed.

She snatched it from Mike's hand before he could even hand it to her and held it out toward John.

"Easy now," Mike said, holding her by the back of the life belt when she slid right up to the edge. He looked at Katy. "Sometimes she gets too close."

After drawing her safely back, Mike accepted a ball from Katy. Sarah made a move to grab it, but he pulled it back.

"Tell me what it is first, Sarah."

"Ba . . ."

"Come on."

"Ball!"

"Right. What color?"

It looked as if Sarah was pulling the words from deep in her throat. "Red."

"Red. Very good." And Mike handed her the ball. "Now throw it to John."

Gus gave John the signal, and when Sarah tossed the ball, he was ready to pop it back deftly with his nose. The little girl squealed happily as it bounced over her head.

Katy moved to retrieve it, her gaze turning up toward the top of the dock. "Yo," she called to Mike, "you better see this."

Katy watched as one of Max Hollister's loyalists handed out leaflets to patients and family members gathered in lawn chairs tucked beneath the overhang of one of the shacks.

"I'll be right back," Mike said, springing to his feet with hot energy dripping off him. "Watch Sarah."

Katy followed him up the dock with her eyes, wondering if he was going to use the fists he held clenched at his sides. He had just reached the man with the leaflets when she heard a splash.

Katy swung and saw Sarah flapping desperately about in the water, her mouth working up and down with no sounds emerging. She continued to thrash, panicked, even though the life belt was holding her above the surface.

Katy jumped in after her, tried to get an arm around the little girl, but Sarah fought her off and drifted further out into the pen. Three of the dolphins began circling them. Katy stayed even, finally latching a hand to the thick rubber of her life belt only to be struck in the eye with a tiny, flailing fist. She refused to let go, joined on with her second hand and tried to tug Sarah back to shore.

But the little girl continued to thrash and kick, resisting all of Katy's efforts to help her. Fingernails raked her cheek and a thumb stabbed her other eye. Katy was vaguely conscious of footsteps pounding down the dock, desperate shouts coming from somewhere. She saw Mike Fontana dive into the water, surfacing almost instantly.

"Let me have her!" he ordered.

Katy pushed herself backwards in the pen, treading water as Mike captured Sarah in a rescue grip beneath her small shoulders. Katy could see the look of angered frustration on his face, the water beading up as if his skin was boiling it.

"I told you to watch her," he snapped, tugging the still struggling Sarah back toward the platform where her mother knelt nervously.

"So it's my fault."

Mike didn't look back at Katy. "Maybe I made a mistake."

"You sure did: You left. Something you're good at, had lots of practice with."

"All you had to do was keep your eyes on—"

"Whose fault was it sixteen years ago? Who'd you blame for walking away then? My mother?"

"I didn't think I was asking too much of you."

Katy started to swim away as Mike reached the platform. "Just once, don't look for somebody else to blame," she said just loud enough for him to hear.

CHAPTER TWENTY-THREE

"I could use your help with something," Mike said to Katy first thing the next morning.

She looked up from the patient folder she was working on in her lap in the shade of a hibiscus tree. "You're the boss," she said and rose to follow him.

Gus Anton had agreed to let Mike use his dolphins, Sonny and Cher, for his language project. Mike dedicated a smaller pen on the center's southern side for the project. The pen had once been a berth where boat repairs had been performed, when Dolphin Key had been a marina. A six-foot channel connected it with the pen where Sonny and Cher lived, and Mike had constructed a gate he opened only when he wanted to do language work with the two dolphins. That way Sonny and Cher were easily able to distinguish what tasks were expected of them.

But this pen, Katy noted, was nothing like the other two carved out of the lagoon. The near side was finished in a pool-like wall, obviously left over from Dolphin Key's days as a marina, along with a concrete deck that workmen had once used as a staging area to repair boats. On that deck lay simple toys like balls and hula hoops amidst high-tech computer panels and monitors encased in plastic to keep them protected from the water. There was also a single stereo speaker mounted on a pedestal and connected to wires that ran beneath the asphalt.

"See, I'm getting ready to submit my application for a grant," Mike explained. "I could use an extra hand for the homestretch."

Katy flapped an upturned palm. "I tend to drop things, remember?"

"This is something you can't break." Mike took a deep breath. "I owe you an apology for how I behaved yesterday. Had a lot on my mind's what it was. See, Joe had cancer a few years ago. He thinks it's come back."

Katy felt a numbness in her head. Something quivered inside her.

"That's why I snapped at you. I'm sorry."

She tried to shrug it off. "No harm done."

"There could have been."

"I didn't know that kid would jump into the water."

"I shouldn't have blamed you, and I shouldn't have left the platform. I'm sorry."

"Imagine where we'd be if you could have said that eighteen years ago."

"That's the point."

Katy looked at him. "Do you think Joe's sick again?"

Mike shrugged. "Swollen gland. It could be almost anything. We'll just have to wait a little while."

"Is that a good idea?"

Mike didn't answer her, suddenly seeming very far away. "It's what he wants."

"You think the dolphins can help him?"

"I hope so."

"But they can't cure cancer, right? That's not what they're about."

"I don't know. Maybe."

Katy hesitated. "How?"

"It's almost like the dolphins look at you and right away know everything that's wrong. Then they zero in and try to fix it."

She recalled her own powerful initial experience, wondered what the dolphins had seen wrong when they looked inside her. "They get into your head and leave stuff behind. Is that it?"

"They leave everything different than it was before. I can't say exactly how. The real experts call it 'cavitation.'"

"Huh?"

"Picture molecules being ripped apart so they can rebuild from scratch. The theory is that's what happens when they echolocate you. You felt it in your bones, all the way through your spine, tearing molecules apart. If you were sick, sometimes, *sometimes*, when the molecules rebuild maybe they do so without cancer, and maybe the tumors shrink or go into remission."

"Does Joe ever see his mother?"

"Not since she walked out. I managed to get in touch with her after he got sick the first time. She spoke to him a few times, sent some get-well cards. Nothing in a couple years at least."

"I should tell Joe I know how that feels."

"I only wish I was the one sick, not him."

"And you could do all my jail time for me."

Mike took a deep breath. "I'm doing what I can."

Katy suddenly felt bad for him, even though she didn't

want to. She looked at the two dolphins swimming round the pen. "So what do you want me to do with these guys?"

Mike followed her gaze. "You think they're smart?"

"I guess."

"But they can't talk to you."

"Makes them even smarter."

"And you can't talk to them."

"No."

"What if you could? What if they could?"

Katy tilted her head to the side. "So you *are* trying to teach them to talk."

"No—communicate. There's a big difference. Look, fundamentally I believe dolphins are as smart as we are. And, that said, it's incredible how little we truly understand about them. How they think, what they think. Swim with them, talk to them, and you'll only hear what you want to."

"What's the alternative?"

"What's the basis of all training?"

"I don't know," Katy said, starting to get intrigued. "I guess teaching them tasks."

"And rewarding them for successfully completing those tasks?"

Katy nodded. In the pen the two dolphins, Sonny and Cher, were hovering closer, heads poked over the surface as if to listen.

"In other words," Mike continued, "we tell the dolphins what we want them to do."

"Yes."

"I take the opposite approach here; the dolphins tell me what they want *me* to do."

Katy trailed Mike closer to the edge of the pen, Sonny and Cher following their every move.

"See that circuit panel attached to the concrete side of the pen underwater?"

Katy nodded. "Looks like a tic-tac-toe board."

"Those are symbols the dolphins have come to equate with various objects they can ask for. Here, I'll give you a little demonstration."

Katy stood back as Mike moved right up to the edge of the pen and summoned the dolphins to him with a loud clap of his hands.

"Play," he said to Sonny.

The dolphin lurched upward enthusiastically and then dove under water, surging for the circuit panel built into the wall. Katy watched him strike one of the nine symbols with his nose.

"*Ball,*" a computer-synthesized voice intoned through the pedestal-mounted speaker.

Mike leaned over and tossed Sonny a ball, which he immediately took underwater and began bouncing against the concrete wall of the pen.

"Play," he said to Cher, and she too darted under water for the circuit panel.

"*Hoop,*" the computer-synthesized voice said after she had struck one of the symbols, and Mike had the hula hoop ready for her by the time she resurfaced.

"Looks like they're teaching you tricks," Katy noted.

"That's the point. But there's a lot more going on. As the dolphins make their choices, we're recording the sounds they're making, trying to establish a cadence and rhythm that might someday yield what is effectively a dolphin dictionary. They get to know our language not only by sound, but also by sign and symbol. And we get to know theirs by the noises they make in response to those signs and symbols. We're talking about a common ground here, the basis on which we can actually establish a direct means of communication between our two species."

Katy looked at Sonny bouncing his ball while Cher tossed her hula hoop into the air and caught it on her nose. "Is this all your grant is about?"

Mike smiled. "No, there's plenty more to it than this." He checked his watch. "But right now we've got to get back to work. Next therapy session starts in five minutes."

"Even more eager than usual, aren't you?"

"I think our patient's ready to speak for the first time. That tends to get me excited."

CHAPTER TWENTY-FOUR

This session Mike decided to try more advanced cognitively based exercises with Stephen Hatch, starting with the colored shapes again.

"Touch the red square," he said, holding a red one in his right hand and blue in his left.

Stephen hesitated and then reached out and touched the red square with two fingers, pulling them away as if the square was hot.

"Very good!" Mike raved, then looked back at Katy. "Getting him to touch objects can help relieve his tactile defensiveness."

"What's that mean?"

"Stephen has a shell around himself," Mike explained, fishing for fresh colored shapes in the milk crate. "Anything he touches or anyone he lets touch him helps him find the way out of it." He turned back to the boy, holding a green square and a green triangle. "Okay, Stephen, let's try something harder. I want you to touch the green square for me."

Stephen Hatch looked quickly from Mike's left hand to his right, seemed confused, and turned his gaze toward the water and the dolphin.

"Look at me, Stephen." Mike waited for the boy's eyes to regard him again, then held out the green square. "We've got to do our work first. We'll go swimming after we do the work. Now, this is the green square." He switched it into his left hand. "I want you to touch it for me."

Stephen reached out to the left but stopped short of touching the square.

"That's it. Now touch it. Come on, reach out a little farther and touch it."

Stephen finally did, very slowly.

"Great! Now we can go swimming? Would you like to go swimming with Sonny?"

The boy started to slide into the water almost too fast for Mike to restrain him. "Wait for me, big guy. . . . That's it."

Gus called Sonny to the platform as Mike wrapped his arms protectively around Stephen. In the water, the boy no longer resisted his touch, his attention rooted so much on the dolphin. He squealed happily as Gus answered Mike's request for a foot push across the lagoon. Only this time, on Mike's instructions, Sonny left them there.

"Where'd he go, Stephen? We'd better call him, we'd better call Sonny. Sonny! Sonny! Come on, say it with me. Sonny." Mike squeezed the boy's cheeks gently. "Son-ny."

Stephen pushed Mike's hand away, and Mike signaled Gus to send Sonny back to pick them up.

On the platform again, Mike asked Katy for a bucket finished in a top fitted with three slots—a square, circle, and triangle tailored to match the shapes he'd been working with. He put the bucket in front of Stephen and then placed a red square into his hand.

"Put the square in the bucket, Stephen."

The boy looked at the bucket, dropped the square.

Mike eased it back into his hand. "Put the square in the bucket."

Stephen dropped it again.

Mike held the square in the boy's grasp this time and maneuvered his tiny hand over the proper slot, releasing it for him. "See. That's all there is to it."

He reached behind him for a pair of the waterproof picture flash cards. He grabbed one in each hand, a shoe and an airplane.

"Which of these do you put on your feet, Stephen?"

The boy didn't seem to be paying attention, then suddenly pointed at the airplane.

Mike made his voice sound joking. "You don't put an airplane on your feet, do you?"

Stephen smiled a little, almost as if he had made a joke.

"Okay, let's try it again. Which of these do you put on your feet?"

This time Stephen pointed at the shoe.

Mike quickly replaced the airplane with a banana and held it up alongside the shoe. "Now, show me something you can eat."

Stephen looked at the flash cards, then looked down again.

"Point to something you can eat, Stephen."

Eyes still on the platform, the boy reached out toward the banana.

"Very good! Want to throw the banana to Sonny?"

Mike eased the wooden card into Stephen's hand and helped him toss it into the lagoon. Gus pointed Sonny toward it and the dolphin circled and pushed it back toward the platform on his nose. Mike helped Stephen reach out into the water and bring the card back onto the platform. Then he grabbed two fresh cards, a dog and a cow.

"Look at me, Stephen. Look at me. . . . Now, which animal goes 'Woof!'? Which animal goes 'Woof!'?"

Stephen slapped the dog with his hand.

Mike switched the cards in his hands. "Now, which animal gives us milk? Which animal gives us milk?"

Stephen started to reach out for the dog again, then changed his mind and slapped the cow.

"Great job! I guess you want to go in the water now, right?"

Stephen started to push toward the water again until Mike fastened his hands on the boy's shoulders. "Tell me you want to go in, Stephen. Say 'in,' " Mike said, exaggerating the enunciation of the word. " 'In,' Stephen. Say 'in.' "

The boy started to lower himself face first toward the water, but Mike stopped him.

"We're not going into the water until you tell me what you want. Until you tell me you want to go in. Come on, say 'in.' "

Stephen began to struggle in his grasp. Mike had Katy take his place holding him and slid into the water, then leaned back over the platform toward the boy who continued trying to fight his way forward.

"Say 'in,' Stephen. That's all you have to do and you can come in the water with me."

The boy's mouth dropped, the motion looking utterly foreign to him, and then narrowed. It looked as if he were trying to speak but no sound emerged.

"Say it with me, Stephen. 'In.' Come on, try your best. 'In.' "

Stephen dropped his mouth again and this time a sound emerged, a kind of soft grunt.

"That's it! You've almost got it! 'In. In.' Just like me. Listen. 'In.' Now together, 'In,' because you want to swim with Sonny."

"In," Stephen said, looking shocked by his own voice. He touched his lips and said the word again, drawing out the *n* sound.

"That was great!"

Katy was so excited she almost let the boy go before Mike was ready. Her father looked up at her, and for that moment everything was right between them, but Mike knew it would take considerably more than a single word to bridge a gap nearly eighteen years in the making.

Gus signaled Sonny to do a series of jumps so the dolphin could show his pleasure as well. After a ball push and slow swim, Mike asked Stephen if he wanted to stay in or get out of the water. Stephen pointed toward Sonny, but Mike eased his hand back.

"That's good, but I want you to tell me. I want you to say 'More.' Can you hear me? 'More.' If you say 'more' I'll know you want to spend more time with the dolphin."

Stephen's mouth dropped again, forming a different shape than before. His face tightened and he sucked in some breath.

"More." Clearer this time.

"Okay," Mike said, smiling wide. "You're the boss."

CHAPTER TWENTY-FIVE

Homer Tiebolt, the old southern lawyer whose granddaughter was in the program, approached Katy after Jilly's session was complete the next day.

"I ever tell you 'bout the time I defended Loralee Gomes?" he asked her.

"Yes," Katy said. "Two days ago."

Homer fingered his pointy chin. "She was a black woman from Clearwater who stabbed a white boy with his own knife when he tried to rape her. The jury was all white, the judge was white, everybody in the courtroom was white except for Loralee, and—"

"Her family was made to sit in the back row," Katy completed.

"Now there hadn't been an acquittal of a black person charged with a crime against a white in this county since I was still in diapers. What I had to do was prove—"

"The white boy was a rapist . . ."

"—before I could even think about forming a defense. So I effectively put him on trial once it became my turn to present my case. 'Cause—"

"If the jury thought he was guilty . . ."

"They would have to find Loralee Gomes innocent. I wasn't just making a case, young lady, I was making history. They still talk about that case in these parts, I tell you. All the way back in sixty-two."

"Four," Katy corrected.

Puzzled, Homer looked at her as if he had just woken up and wasn't sure where he was. "What'd I say?"

"Two."

"Right," he agreed, forgetting the last part of the story, which she knew by heart anyway.

After separating herself from Homer, Katy found Joe eating his lunch at a picnic table set under the shade of a larger canopy near one of the shacks.

"Mind if I join you?"

He looked up at her, then back at his sandwich. The lump on his neck had shrunk considerably, all but gone from what she could tell. "You don't call me little bro anymore."

"I didn't think you liked it," Katy said.

"Dad told you, didn't he?"

"About how you had cancer?"

"Anyway, he told you and you stopped calling me little bro, like you were scared hurting my feelings might make me sicker."

She sat down across from him. "I don't have as much to say when I'm not angry."

"You were angry with me before?"

"I was angry with a whole lot of things. Still am. But I was angry with you because, hey, we've got the same father and you were the one he stuck around."

Joe almost laughed. "Want to trade places?"

"Remember I told you the Dade Flood wouldn't take me back now?"

He perked up. "Because of something you didn't do, you said. Some big secret."

"Wanna hear it?"

Joe abandoned his sandwich and leaned forward.

"The initiation process only starts the process of really being part of the gang. You're not really made until you bleed somebody."

"Huh?"

"Bleed somebody. With a gun or a knife. In a fight, on a drive-by, a cap-ass, or a re-tal."

"What's that?"

"Retaliation," Katy told him. "So one afternoon they put a gun in my hand, stuffed me in the backseat next to the window, and told me it was time to come into the world. We were going hunting. Some high school bitch who had eyes for one of the made girls' boyfriend. Broad daylight. A McDonald's in the burbs where she went with her friends after school."

Joe swallowed hard.

"They had everything scoped out, planned to the minute. We circle the block, waiting. Finally, one of the girls sees the mark getting out of a car and reaches across me to open the window. She was wearing a skirt and had these really long legs. I remember she was smiling and the gun felt heavy and cold in my hand. I started to raise it, had her dead in my sights, but I couldn't pull the trigger.

"I heard someone in the car yelling, 'Shoot! Shoot!,' and the girl must have heard it too, because she turned and looked at me. Our eyes met, but I don't think she ever saw the gun. But one of her friends did and screamed, and the next thing I know we're hauling ass out of there and I'm already getting the crap kicked out of me still in the car.

"So they threw me out of the gang, left me swollen and bloody in the street," Katy said, smiling slightly. "I wasn't even good enough for them."

"I know the feeling," Joe told her.

"I thought you might."

"It's different, though."

"But I'll tell you what's the same. Until a few weeks ago I figured the biggest mistake I ever made was not pulling the trigger. All I had to do was nail that bitch and at least I'd have a place, a home."

"So?"

"So, little bro, now I found a different one. And if this place can do that for an asshole like me, I figure you've got nothing to worry about."

Joe started to shake his head and then looked across the table at her. "You really think so?"

"Wouldn't have said it if I didn't. And, hey, I'm impartial on the subject."

"Not anymore," Joe told her, letting himself smile.

CHAPTER TWENTY-SIX

Mike hoped making Katy his assistant in the dolphin language program would help push their relationship over the difficult hump on which it seemed stuck. Things not any worse between them, but not any better either. He knew she would show up every morning now, just as he knew she'd leave harboring the same bitterness and resentment he could not make her relinquish.

The problem, Mike had realized, was that he was seeing her as the person he wanted her to be, the most recent to be saved under the benevolent auspices of Mike Fontana. He collected the broken and the beaten like toys on a shelf, to be repaired and repainted before going back on display. Found success in their successes, triumph in their triumphs.

But Katy wasn't a patient and, clearly, treating her like one was not getting their relationship where he wanted it to be. Then again, the problem was that he couldn't say exactly where he wanted it to be. The definition eluded him, the goals were unfocused. Children came to Dolphin Key with specific needs Mike could write down on a form to follow their progress. His problems with Katy, on the other hand, fit in no line on any form he had ever seen. Their relationship was based solely on the duties required at Dolphin Key. When they were alone together, no client between them, neither knew what to say to the other, and the days inevitably began and ended in silence.

Mike needed the kind of breakthrough with Katy he had gotten with Zachary Haas that morning, just one day after the boy had successfully completed his first swimming lesson. Still in search of ways to make Zach more willing to use his prostheses, Mike had brought him to the seawater rehabilitation pool.

"Why are we going all the way over here?" Zach asked.

"To meet Sunset Sam."

"I like George."

"You'll like Sunset Sam, too. There's something he can do that George can't."

"What?"

"You'll see."

What Zach saw was the paint, brushes, and canvases Mike had set near the edge of the saltwater pool.

Mike laid down the bucket of fish. He was about to click the water when Sunset Sam surfaced before him. Mike fed him a herring and leaned over the side.

"Wanna show Zach how you paint?"

Then, with the boy looking on in awe, Mike dipped a moistened brush in some paint and held it out so Sunset Sam could grab its tip in his mouth. Mike stole a glance at Katy and could see she was similarly impressed, the kind of look on her face he only saw at times like this. Then he turned back to Sunset Sam and moved the canvas to within reach of the brush. Almost instantly, the dolphin began scrawling an impressionistic design across its surface, flexing his head up, down, and side to side to create the painting.

"Wow," Zach and Katy said, almost together. She smiled at him, and Mike wanted to freeze the expression so he could hold on to it forever.

"Your turn," he said to Zach, easing the canvas away from Sunset Sam, who reluctantly gave up his paintbrush.

The boy looked a bit puzzled until Katy produced the harness fitted with his arm prosthesis from behind her back. Zach enthusiastically let Mike strap the harness on, and Katy worked the paintbrush into a tailored slot at the end of one of the arm extensions. The boy tested its motion, moving the brush with deft shifts of his shoulder.

"I'm ready," Zach said, and Katy held a canvas up before him, while Sunset Sam went back to work on his as well, this time using a new brush and different color of paint.

Mike had a stack of paperwork to catch up on and he'd grudgingly decided to work public swims into the schedule, which meant rearranging a bunch of appointments. His session with Zachary Haas ended at eleven, leaving him nearly two hours of office time, so he could at least get started. But at noon he walked outside, deciding to join Katy and Joe for lunch. He had just drawn within sight of the picnic table they shared beneath the canopy when he noticed Gus Anton loading a pellet rifle on the far platform in the larger pen. Mike figured he could still get there before Gus started firing at the birds lounging on the fence rail, and he started onto the dock.

"Mr. Fontana?" a voice said.

Mike turned and saw a man crush out a cigarette beneath a scuffed shoe on the grass of the shoreline. "That's right. And there's no smoking here."

"Sorry." The man worked an envelope from the pocket of his suit jacket and handed it to Mike. "You have been duly served, sir," he said, and walked off.

CHAPTER TWENTY-SEVEN

"This isn't good, mombo," Jacardi Benoit said in Mike's office, after completing his second reading of the papers Mike had been served with just hours before. They'd tried closing the door for privacy. But the heat built up fast, so Mike had opened it halfway. "This isn't good at all."

"Can you tell me what it means?"

"I'm no lawyer, mahn."

"Take a guess," Mike said. A map of the world hung on the wall before him, full of small tacks marking the homes of all the families who came to Dolphin Key. Lots of states and a number of countries, too. Mike looked at the map and imagined the tacks gone, tiny holes all that would be left of his dream.

Jacardi shrugged and flipped to the third page of the summons. "First of all, the bastard Hollister has got a date in district court for a hearing to determine whether you have violated the Marine Mammal Protection Act."

"Bullshit!" Mike seethed. "How much time do we have?"

"Two months; the hearing's in late September."

"Gives us some time, anyway."

"No, it doesn't, mombo." Jacardi flipped to another page. "See, this complaint here claims the dolphins are in imminent danger and, as a result, this center should be shut down and put under the control of a custodian."

"What in hell does that mean?"

"Someone who makes sure the dolphins are taken care of until the trial."

"I'm out, in other words."

"For good, if you lose the trial."

Mike felt dizzy. He was glad he was sitting down because it felt like someone had sucked out his air with a vacuum cleaner. Life without Dolphin Key was a dark void haunted by phantoms. Like Scrooge when visited by ghosts showing the shadows of what might be. Joe without the dolphins, no second chance with Katy. A grave and a jail cell.

"This is the same thing Hollister pulled in South Carolina." Mike managed to push the words through the quaking of his thoughts.

"But why start with you in Florida?"

"Because I'm an easy target," Mike replied, heat building beneath his flesh. His face felt as if he'd been out in the sun too long and his fingers tingled. "Because he figures I can't afford to fight back."

"Got to show cause for the motion to be denied at this preliminary hearing in ten days, mahn."

Mike laid his beefy hands palms down on the desk. The backs were fiery red. "And how much is that gonna cost me?"

"More than you got."

"Not necessarily," said a voice from the doorway.

What remained of Homer Tiebolt's hair had been blown out to the sides by the wind. He looked to Mike to be out of breath and leaned against the door frame before continuing.

"What I mean is, I'd be happy to be of service to you, especially after all you've done for my granddaughter. Least I can do, from my perspective."

Mike exchanged a quick glance with Jacardi. "How'd you find out I needed a lawyer?"

"You want to quibble about details, son, or you want to get down to business?"

Homer read the twelve-page complaint while sitting in Mike's chair.

"A damn frivolous suit, that's what this is," he said, slapping the pages down on the blotter when he was finished. "Pure harassment."

"It worked in South Carolina," Mike told him.

"And the dolphin therapy center up there compares to Dolphin Key how exactly?"

"They ran it out of an old aquarium."

Homer's eyes blinked, sharpened. "And why did this aquarium close?" His voice sounder surer, stronger.

"I have no idea."

"Could it be the original aquarium closed because its facilities were woefully inadequate, a fact that was of little concern to the new tenants Hollister subsequently went after?"

"I wouldn't know."

"Neither would I," said Homer, out of his lawyerly cadence. "But it makes sense, doesn't it? Even you have spoken out about the way a lot of captive dolphins are treated."

"True."

"If asked to testify in the South Carolina case, whose side would you have been on?"

"Good question."

"So Max Hollister had a point."

"He did there. He doesn't here."

"There's a difference between the two centers, then."

"Only night and day."

Homer Tiebolt rose out of the chair, knees cracking. Mike heard a scratching sound as the old man's Bermuda shorts peeled away from the vinyl.

"Exactly," the old lawyer said. "So precedent's irrelevant in this case. Hollister has to prove his argument purely on its own merits as it applies to Dolphin Key."

Mike exchanged a glance with Jacardi, his face feeling cooler. "So how do we fight him?"

Homer was silent for a time, so long that Mike thought his mind might have strayed elsewhere. "Well, Hollister is putting a lot of emphasis on this motion to be heard in ten days to have a custodian appointed for the center. He thought he could blindside you, get the motion hearing on the docket quicker than you could mount an adequate defense. My advice would be we turn the tables. We turn this preliminary hearing into a street fight and make sure we're the ones standing when it's over."

"When was the last time you tried a case, Mr. Tiebolt?"

"Never defended a dolphin before in my life."

"How about the last time with a man?"

"Nineteen eighty-eight. Not that it matters."

"It doesn't?"

"This case isn't about a man, even you, Mike; it's about dolphins. And the more we keep it about dolphins, *your* dolphins, the better chance we stand of the judge denying Hollister's motion in ten days' time." Homer Tiebolt stood up as straight as he could. "Now, any other questions?"

THREE

CHAPTER TWENTY-EIGHT

"All rise!"

For Katy the scene was too familiar. Same building, same courtroom that was blistering hot in the areas the air conditioner didn't quite reach. And, she realized with no small degree of shock, Celine Rosenthal would be presiding. The gruff, no-nonsense judge who had sentenced her to two years of jail time.

"Be seated!"

"All right, counsels," the judge began in the same harsh tone Katy recalled all too well, "this preliminary hearing is being conducted under the stipulations and procedures set forth in the Marine Mammal Protection Act. Its purpose is to determine whether the violations of such act, alleged against the Dolphin Key Center for Dolphin Human Therapy, are grievous enough to warrant this court granting the complainant's motion to appoint a custodian in the period before trial. Mr. Moss, is the complainant ready to proceed?"

Katy watched Arlan Moss, a top-notch litigator with his own Miami cable television show and courtside seats at Heat games, rise smoothly.

"We are, Your Honor."

He was in his mid-thirties, outfitted in a well-tailored,

cream-colored suit. His hair was slicked back, and he wore glasses he didn't seem to need. Katy doubted he had ever dropped a bead of sweat.

"Is the defendant ready to proceed?"

Homer Tiebolt's hands trembled as he sorted through the slim pile of papers he had pulled from a fawn-colored briefcase. The zipper was broken and the leather was cracked and blotched with water stains. Homer had come dressed in a suit that smelled of mothballs and carried closet dust on both lapels. The old man's tie was knotted much too thickly and only reached the center of his shirt.

"Is the defendant ready to proceed?" the judge repeated.

Homer bounced up out of his chair, as if hit by an electric shock. "Homer Tiebolt for the defense, Your Honor."

"I'm aware of that, counsel. Are you ready to proceed?"

"Of course, Your Honor."

"All right, Mr. Moss, call your first witness."

Moss rose smoothly out of his chair again. "Your Honor, we call Max Hollister to the stand."

Hollister took the witness stand and was sworn in. He'd tied his stringy hair into a ponytail, and the bright courtroom lights showed every one of the lines on his parched face.

Arlan Moss checked the yellow legal pad beneath him and began. "Mr. Hollister, you are a dolphin trainer, are you not?"

"I was. I'm not any longer."

"I stand corrected. How long *were* you a dolphin trainer?"

"Over twenty-five years."

"You have a degree in marine biology?"

"A doctorate."

"Very impressive, sir. And what led you into the field of dolphin training?"

"Study, at first. I had secured a number of grants to research the capacity of dolphins to communicate directly with man. When the grants ran out, I moved into the field I was most suited for."

"And your credits include . . ."

"Seaworld, Hershey Park in Pennsylvania, Disney, Universal Studios."

Mike watched Arlan Moss respond with rehearsed surprise. His eyelids fluttered in feigned consternation. "It would seem your more recent avocation represents quite a change of heart."

"It evolved over a number of years," Hollister responded.

"In fact, it would not be an exaggeration to say you are perhaps the foremost, and certainly the most outspoken, critic of parks and centers which keep dolphins in captivity, would it?"

"I don't know about foremost; I would agree with outspoken. I've been jailed five times for protesting."

"Protesting what you yourself helped to foster."

Hollister's expression lengthened. His eyes found Mike's briefly. He shifted his ponytail behind him.

"I think," Hollister said finally, "my protests are rooted in the level of blame I bear for all this. In the years 1994 to 1998, almost two hundred dolphins were registered as captive in Florida by centers both legitimate and otherwise under federal requirements set down in the Marine Mammal Protection Act."

Moss retreated to his table and retrieved a set of stapled pages.

"Is this a complete list?" he asked Hollister.

Hollister examined the list quickly. "It looks to be."

Moss ambled across the courtroom and placed the pages before the clerk. "Plaintiffs' A, your Honor."

"So noted," said Rosenthal, accepting the pages from the clerk. "Please proceed, Mr. Moss."

"And could you explain, Mr. Hollister, what those highlighted portions mean?"

"That a dolphin is now deceased."

"And how many of the two hundred are highlighted?"

"One hundred and twenty-two."

A collective gasp fluttered through the courtroom.

Arlan Moss looked to be gasping, too. "You're telling me that *sixty* percent of captive dolphins died in this four-year period."

"That we know of."

"What do you mean?"

"That it's possible there are far more who perished in centers which chose *not* to respond to the mandates spelled out in the law."

"And what are some of the leading causes of these deaths, Mr. Hollister?"

"Pneumonia, liver disorders, immune-system breakdowns, suicide."

Arlan Moss leaned forward dramatically at that, skepticism painted over his empty face. "Did you say 'suicide'?"

"I did, sir. For dolphins, breathing is a voluntary response, not involuntary as is the case with humans. I am quite convinced that a number of dolphin deaths in captivity are directly related to the animal sadly losing its desire to live."

"And these suicides you insist took place, did they occur mostly at poorly kept facilities?"

"On the contrary," said Hollister, "a number of them occurred in the best aquariums, where the care the animals received was absolutely top-notch."

"And did you ever witness firsthand what in your estimation was a dolphin suicide?"

"I did," Hollister answered, swallowing hard. "And it was my fault."

"Did you mistreat this dolphin, Mr. Hollister?"

"I guess you could call it mistreatment. I see that now; I didn't then. After all, she was well fed, well cared for, lived like royalty. It wasn't enough."

"You're suggesting, then, that top-notch care, in and of itself, is not enough to ward off disease and, in some cases, even suicide."

"That's right. These are wild animals. They are not meant to be kept in captivity under any circumstances."

"And this is why you have dedicated your life to abolishing the practice you helped pioneer."

"Yes, sir, that is correct."

Arlan Moss turned toward the judge. "No further questions, Your Honor."

"Mr. Tiebolt," the judge signaled.

The courtroom had one wall of windows, and a shaft of sizzling hot light streaming in seemed to trap Homer in his chair. The old man, Mike feared, would remain a prisoner until the judge repeated his name louder and then, having not taken a single note, would stumble through his cross-examination until he forgot who he was questioning altogether. Mike felt his world exploding from the inside out. He was wondering if he should rise and question Hollister himself, when Homer sprang up and cleared his throat.

"Just a few questions, Mr. Hollister," he said from their

table, loud and sharp, his deep voice carrying through the courtroom without benefit of the microphone. The sun had left a line of sweat across his brow, and Homer wiped it with a handkerchief. "Are you acquainted with my client, Mike Fontana?"

"Slightly."

"But you're not personally acquainted with him."

"We're not socially friendly, if that's what you mean."

"And you've never even visited the Dolphin Key Center for Dolphin Human Therapy."

"No."

"In fact, it's my understanding you've never actually viewed a session with a patient; that, in fact, you've only viewed the facility from the parking lot. Is that correct, sir?"

"Yes," said Hollister, "it is."

Homer shook his head, his turn for the dramatic now. "Mr. Hollister, are you even able to point out Mike Fontana in this courtroom today?"

"I—"

"No, strike that." Homer laid his hands on the table and leaned forward. His knees wobbled. Mike could hear both his elbows crack audibly. "Mr. Hollister, that list of registered dolphins your lawyer gave to the court that included the deaths of a large percentage of dolphins registered under the Marine Mammal Protection Act. Did any of these deaths occur at Dolphin Key?"

"One, I believe."

"And the cause, Mr. Hollister?"

"I believe it was a preexisting medical condition."

"Preexisting to what?"

"The animal's rescue."

"Rescue?"

"I believe it had beached itself."

Homer gripped the table tighter. His mouth dropped and quivered. His eyes hung open. Mike felt the grasp of panic, started to slide as subtly as possible toward the old man when his eyelids fluttered and, just like that, he was alert again.

"Mr. Hollister, are you aware of how many dolphins have resided at Dolphin Key since its inception almost three years ago?"

"No, sir."

"I didn't think so. Would it surprise you to learn that the answer is fifteen, fifteen different dolphins?"

Hollister didn't respond.

"Are you aware that of these fifteen, only eight have ever been utilized in the therapy program?"

"I don't see what—"

"Are you further aware that those dolphins who remain in the therapy program at Dolphin Key all have medical conditions which would make their return to the wild both unwise and perhaps negligent?"

Hollister swallowed hard.

"And would you, sir, deem one death from a preexisting medical condition to be an acceptable ratio in view of these facts?"

Hollister shifted uneasily. "No dolphin death is acceptable."

"Of course, it isn't. I'm sorry." Homer Tiebolt walked out from behind the table, and Mike got the same feeling he did when he watched a swimmer venture too far away from shore. "Now, if we were to accept your theory that dolphins are capable of suicide . . ."

"It's not just my theory."

". . . then we would be acknowledging their ability to

make decisions, choices based on emotional responses to their environment. Would that be correct?"

"I couldn't have said it better myself."

"Sometimes they make the choice to die, to end their lives voluntarily, when they are unhappy and/or mistreated?"

"All too often, I'm afraid."

Homer Tiebolt swooped in close, his trap sprung. "Then, sir, how do you explain the fact that, by your own admission, no dolphin at Dolphin Key has ever made such a choice?"

Hollister had no answer.

Homer looked up at the judge. "No further questions, Your Honor."

CHAPTER TWENTY-NINE

The next witness was Dr. Rima Firrone, a nationally renowned marine veterinarian who had helped craft the Marine Mammal Protection Act for the government and who continued to serve on the federal board overseeing its implementation. Arlan Moss returned to the podium, looking a little less cocky and sure after Homer's cross-examination of Max Hollister, Mike thought.

"Dr. Firrone, opposing counsel is making much out of the fact that no dolphin has ever taken its own life at Dolphin Key. Is this fact relevant, so far as the standards laid down by the Marine Mammal Protection Act is concerned?"

"No, it is not."

"And why is that, Doctor?" Moss used a quick toss of his head to aim the question toward Homer Tiebolt at the same time.

"Because mistreatment is not limited to cruelty or abuse. Mistreatment can also mean making the animal dependent on man for its survival. Rendering it incapable of returning to the wild."

"Even if it wanted to make such a return?"

"It's doubtful it would want to, if all its basic necessities are being tended to. Especially feeding. The true tragedy is that after enough time has elapsed, the animal may not be able to survive in the wild anymore, even if it tried to."

"What does this say about the rehabilitation of sick dolphins?"

"That it's a sham, an excuse to keep them and turn them into a sideshow. Rehabilitation causes dependence, and dependence means the animal can never again flourish in its own environment."

Moss flipped the page on his legal pad of notes. "Dr. Firrone, you have been especially critical of so-called dolphin petting zoos, swim parks, and even therapy centers. Could you explain why?"

"Because forced interaction with humans causes great stress to the animal. Much has been written about the unique bond dolphins share with us. But there is no evidence whatsoever to support it. On the contrary, all available evidence indicates the onset of stress-related disorders to be in direct proportion to the number and duration of forced encounters with humans."

"In the case of Dolphin Human Therapy, also known as Dolphin Assisted Therapy, though, that would seem an acceptable cost."

"Except there is also no empirical evidence, not a single shred of proof, that such therapy works. Or, if it does, that it works any better than similar therapies using horses, dogs, cats, even hamsters and mice. I am not suggesting that some people have not been and continue to be helped in some ways by swimming with dolphins. But the suggestion that dolphins are able to effect miracle cures has led to more and more of them being captured in the wild to serve that end. And the apparent benefits, the sanctity of the cause, has led those charged with enforcing the Marine Mammal Protection Act to look the other way and neglect their duties."

"And yet, Dr. Firrone, you have expressed few negative remarks regarding dolphin performance shows at facilities like Seaworld."

Firrone shook the hair from her face before responding. "Because these dolphins only perform a few hours a day under very precise and regulated conditions, and they are not forced to have direct interaction with humans, other than their trainers. Dolphins involved at therapy centers, on the other hand, work far longer and are subjected to countless hours of often poorly supervised human interaction with no real regulation whatsoever."

"And until proper regulations are in place?"

"These centers should be closed down without exception."

"No further questions, Your Honor," said Arlan Moss.

Homer Tiebolt was out of his chair before Moss had finished his sentence, had begun his questioning while his opponent was still gathering his notes at the podium. "Dr. Firrone, I'd like to clear something up, if I may. Federal law now prohibits the capture of any dolphin in the wild. Is that correct?"

"That doesn't mean there—"

"Yes or no, please, Doctor."

"Yes."

"So anyone who captures a dolphin at sea, for whatever reason, would be guilty of a federal crime."

"Yes," Firrone said, almost reluctantly.

"Dr. Firrone, was not the participation of large aquariums, where dolphin performances are central, crucial in drafting the Marine Mammal Protection Act?"

"We had their cooperation, if that's what you mean. They felt it was in their best interests as well."

"I'm sure they did," Homer said, a sharp edge of sarcasm lacing his voice. "Now would it surprise you to learn that the dolphins at these centers are usually considered the top draw and are directly responsible for generating between five hundred million and one billion dollars per year in income?"

"No, it would not."

"And would it surprise you to learn, Doctor, that income generated by all dolphin therapy centers combined barely approaches one million dollars per year?"

"I hope it goes no higher."

"I'm sure you do, just as I'm sure you hope the income of aquariums and theme parks featuring dolphins goes no lower, because of its impact on local economies."

Moss started to rise. "Your Honor—"

But Homer kept rolling, changing the subject fast enough to quiet his opponent and keep the judge from intervening. "Doctor, a few minutes ago you stated that interaction with humans causes dolphins great stress, which contributes in large measure to their problems living in captivity. Would that be an accurate paraphrase?"

"Quite."

"And have you done tests to back your conclusion up?"

"No, but the prevailing data more than supports it, in the absence of such studies."

"But do you have any data with which to compare that? You don't, do you?"

"I'm afraid I don't understand the question, sir."

"A life in the wild. Foraging for food, avoiding nets and the hooks of sport fishermen, finding familiar waters polluted and uninhabitable. The life of the wild dolphin in its environment. Would you describe that as stressful?"

"I'd describe it as their natural habitat."

"That doesn't answer my question. Is the life I have just described stressful?"

"I wouldn't know."

"There's no prevailing data, is there? So when you describe the lives of dolphins around man as stressful, you fail to consider that their lives in the wild could be, very likely are, even more stressful. Is that not a fact?"

Firrone squeezed her lips together, smudging her lipstick. Her face turned a similar shade of red. "I really couldn't say."

"But you have stated, Doctor, that there is no empirical evidence to support the reported success of Dolphin Human Therapy. Is that correct?"

"Yes."

Homer removed a manila folder from his briefcase and laid it open before him on the table. Then he fished through a number of pockets in his jacket before locating his glasses.

"I take it then, Doctor, that you are not familiar with a study conducted by Dr. David Nathanson entitled 'Long-Term Effectiveness of Dolphin-Assisted Therapy for Children with Severe Disabilities.' "

"That is hardly a representative study."

Homer read on, holding his glasses on his nose. " 'The research subjects numbered seventy-one sets of parents from eight different countries over a three-year period.' *Seventy-one*, doctor."

"Yes, but—"

"What about 'Effectiveness of Short-Term Dolphin-Assisted Therapy for Children with Severe Disabilities?' Are you familiar with that study, also conducted by Dr. Nathanson?"

Firrone swallowed hard. "No."

"Forty-seven children, ages two to thirteen," Homer read. "Nineteen with cerebral palsy, eleven with brain damage, five with Down's syndrome, four with autism, two with Angleman, two with Rett syndrome, two with tuberous sclerosis, one with Cri-du-chat, and one with a head injury. Wouldn't you call that representative, Dr. Firrone?"

"Objection!" Arlan Moss shouted before Firrone had a chance to respond. "Your Honor, even if these minor, professionally unrecognized studies were accurate, they are not relevant to the work being specifically carried out at Dolphin Key."

"In that case, Your Honor, I have further documentation I am prepared to enter into evidence," Homer said, pulling from his old briefcase the thick stack of folders he had wedged in that morning. Mike held his breath as a few of the top folders got stuck in the zipper. Homer left manila strands in the teeth when he yanked them free. "Permission to approach, Your Honor."

"Granted."

Homer gathered up the folders and started across the floor. His arms trembled from the exertion and Mike could see his legs were getting shaky, too. His locomotion worsened the further he drew from the table, having lost the security of something to lean on in the twenty-foot chasm between the pews and Judge Rosenthal. Mike watched Homer work his body sideways against the bench when he got there, taking some of the pressure off before he raised the stack of folders overhead and plopped them down on the clerk's desk.

"Your Honor, in addition to studies conducted by Dr. David Nathanson, we are presenting these files of patients involved in the Dolphin Key program into evidence."

"Defendant's A and B for identification," the judge said, barely able to suppress her smile at Homer's shrewd work as she accepted the pile of folders at the bench from the clerk. "Continue, Mr. Tiebolt."

"Thank you, Your Honor. Now, Dr. Firrone, let us return our attention to the dolphin population of Dolphin Key. Do you recall the total number of dolphins to have resided at the center since its inception?"

"I believe it was fifteen."

"What about how many are currently in residence?"

"That I wouldn't know."

"The number is seven, including a recently rescued male." Homer stroked his chin dramatically. "So we have seven in residence, one transferred, and one unfortunate death." He tightened his focus on Rima Firrone once more. "Doctor, what happened to the other six?"

"I wouldn't know."

"Would it surprise you to learn that those six were released back into their natural habitats?"

"That doesn't mean they're thriving. Or that they're even still alive," Dr. Firrone protested.

"But they didn't come back, did they? And all were freeze-branded on their dorsal fins with liquid nitrogen prior to being released, and none of those have turned up again."

"That doesn't prove anything."

Homer waited a moment before responding. "It proves they're not dead."

Moss called four more witnesses, each of whom strengthened his case slightly in spite of Homer Tiebolt's brilliant parrying.

But in no way did their testimony ensure that the motion to appoint a custodian to take over Dolphin Key would be upheld.

"Mr. Tiebolt," the judge said, after making some notes, "given the lateness of the hour, would the defense like to begin presenting its case tomorrow?"

"No, Your Honor, we'd prefer to get to it now. I have a witness waiting in the hall."

"Proceed then."

"Your Honor, the defense calls Zachary Haas to the stand."

CHAPTER THIRTY

The doors to the courtroom opened, and Zachary Haas's mother wheeled him down the center aisle, drawing stares and muffled comments from those squeezed into the rows.

"Your Honor," roared Arlan Moss, "I must strenuously object to this display!"

"On what grounds, Mr. Moss?"

Moss realized his blunder too late to correct it and simply sat back down with a shrug. For his part, Zachary Haas gazed shyly about the courtroom, smiling at Mike when he passed the defense table. His mother backed his wheelchair up against the witness stand.

"Zachary," said Judge Rosenthal, "do you understand the difference between the truth and a lie?"

"Sure I do."

"And do you also understand you must tell only the truth in this courtroom today?"

The boy nodded.

"Proceed, Mr. Tiebolt."

"Permission to approach the witness, Your Honor."

"Granted."

"Hi, Zachary," Homer said as he shuffled forward.

"Hi."

Homer stopped and pointed at Mike Fontana. "Do you know that man, Zachary?"

"Yes, it's Mike."

"Do you like him?"

"Sure."

"Why?"

Zach rotated his upper body nervously from side to side. "Because he helps me."

"How does he help you?"

"He lets me play with the dolphins, do stuff with one named George."

"What kind of stuff?"

"Feed him—I mean her—throw a ball back and forth, swim and, oh yeah, last week we painted."

"You painted with the dolphin?"

"A different dolphin, a new one. He painted, then I painted. We used different brushes."

Homer drew right up to Zach's wheelchair and rested his hand on one of the arm guards. "Had you ever thrown a ball before you came to Dolphin Key and met Mike Fontana?"

"No."

"Had you ever swum before?"

"No."

"Had you ever painted?"

Zachary shook his head.

Homer lowered his voice a little. "Do you understand why you're here today, Zachary?"

"A little."

"Why are you here?"

"Mike needs my help."

"And how can you help him?"

"By telling everybody what he and the dolphins have done for me."

"Just one more question, Zachary: Are you happier since you've been coming to Dolphin Key?"

"Oh, yes," the boy said, nodding resolutely. "Oh, yes."

Homer looked up at Judge Rosenthal. "No further questions, Your Honor."

"Mr. Moss?" the judge said.

Moss drummed his fingers on the table, weighing his options in view of the recent outburst that had clearly cost him. "No questions, Your Honor," he said finally.

Judge Rosenthal looked pleased, her eyes back on Homer Tiebolt, as Zachary's mother started to wheel him back down the center of the courtroom.

"Mr. Tiebolt, do you have any other witnesses to present?"

The old man seemed lost in another fugue, a bad one, when his spine suddenly straightened and he cleared his throat to ready his voice.

"I do, Your Honor."

"Proceed, then."

"Your Honor, the defense recalls Max Hollister."

CHAPTER THIRTY-ONE

Hollister's eyes fell on Homer Tiebolt, as he rose and made his way across the courtroom to the witness stand again.

Homer started to step out from behind the table, but his legs wobbled and he grabbed the edge for support, holding his ground.

"The witness is reminded that he is still under oath," the judge cautioned. "You may proceed, Mr. Tiebolt."

Homer gripped the edge of the table hard. "You don't mind taking the stand again, do you, Mr. Hollister?" he began, his strong voice belying the weak spell that seemed on the verge of overtaking his body.

"Not at all."

"And why is that?"

"Because I stand behind my actions. I believe in everything I've done. I believe it's all justified."

"In your eyes."

"Dolphins should not be enslaved, should not be removed from their natural environments to do the bidding of man."

"So you think that's what this hearing is about."

"This hearing, sir, is about preventing man from taking undue advantage of another species."

As Mike watched, he thought Homer Tiebolt's hands suddenly got a little stronger. "But you haven't made a case for cats and dogs here today."

"No, I haven't."

"Then you make a distinction between dolphins and other animals."

"Of course."

"Why?"

"Because dogs and cats are domesticated. They are bred to be house pets."

"But not dolphins."

Hollister's expression turned theatrically sad. "My own experience proves that."

"And, as Dr. Firrone has pointed out, other assisted therapy programs involve other animals, like horses. Have you targeted them too, Mr. Hollister?"

"Not at all."

"Why? Do they have the empirical evidence to substantiate claims dolphin therapy cannot?"

"They don't need it."

"Why absolve these other programs?"

"Because those animals belong among men," Hollister said, rolling his eyes in increased frustration.

"But not dolphins."

"They are intelligent creatures of high order, Mr. Tiebolt. And there is plenty of data and plenty of studies to support that."

"Is there?"

"I can recommend some good books." Another smirk. "I wrote two myself."

"Too bad the dolphins can't read them, too."

"Who says they can't?" Hollister responded, and the crowd squeezed into the courtroom chuckled.

Mike watched Homer let go of the table edge and venture out in front of it, looking very much like a tightrope walker working without a net. "Then you are stating—are you not?— that dolphins are more intelligent than other so-called domesticated animals; that they are in essence capable of cognitive decision-making abilities. Able to learn, communicate with one other, and experience powerful emotions."

"Yes, I've already admitted all that." Hollister leaned confidently back in the witness chair.

"Where is this going, Mr. Tiebolt?" the judge asked, her clear impatience giving an edge to her words.

"To the point, Your Honor." He addressed the court now, instead of Max Hollister. "We have heard from a number of informative witnesses today, all except the ones who matter the most."

"Who else have we yet to hear from, Mr. Tiebolt?"

Homer waited for Mike Fontana to nod before responding. "The dolphins of Dolphin Key, Your Honor. And I intend to call them as my next witnesses."

CHAPTER THIRTY-TWO

"Dolphins, Mr. Tiebolt? Did I hear you right?" Judge Rosenthal asked, leaning forward over the bench. "You want to call dolphins to the stand?"

"They are the true defendants in this case, Your Honor. And by the complainants' own admission, their intelligence puts them above dogs, cats, and any other animals. I respectfully ask that my request be granted."

"Your Honor!" Arlan Moss was on his feet by then, different shades of color pumping in and out of his formless face. "Can we please put an end to this farce?"

The judge admonished Moss with a flap of her small hand. "Not so fast, Mr. Moss. I want to hear how Mr. Tiebolt intends to call witnesses incapable of speaking."

"Dolphins can't speak as we understand speech, of course, Your Honor. But they can communicate. And experiments have been undertaken by Mr. Fontana at Dolphin Key to teach the dolphins to use our language to communicate." Homer cocked an eye back toward Mike. "I'm sure Mr. Fontana can explain how—"

"I'll take you at your word that a suitable demonstration can be arranged for the court's enlightenment."

"And will opposing counsel have the opportunity to cross-examine these witnesses?" asked Moss, smirking.

"So long as you allow for certain restrictions with your language and word choice, yes," Homer replied.

Moss hadn't looked ready for that answer. "Your Honor, I must object to this entire display. The notion of dolphins somehow answering questions put to them presupposes a conditioned response. The dolphin will answer what it has been trained to answer without using any purported cognitive skills whatsoever."

Homer remained undeterred. "I would bring the court's attention to the case of *Reynolds vs. Hennessey Medical* in which a chimpanzee trained in the use of sign language was permitted to testify in its own behalf at a trial to determine the animal's custody. I would further submit that custodial issues come to the heart of this case and thus dolphins should be afforded the same rights as man—and chimp—in determining their futures."

"Your Honor!" objected Arlan Moss.

"This is a hearing, Mr. Moss. Were it a trial I would be inclined to agree with you. But under the circumstances I see no harm in listening to what these animals have to tell us." The judge laced her fingers beneath her chin. "However, your concerns about preconditioned, trained responses are justified."

"If I may expand on that point, Your Honor," Moss requested, calm again.

"Proceed, Mr. Moss."

"The participation of Mr. Fontana eliminates any confidence the court could have in such a demonstration and its relative importance to the case at hand. I would thus argue that any 'questioning' be done without Mr. Fontana serving as intermediary in order to provide the demonstration with at least some degree of credibility and impartiality."

Judge Rosenthal nodded, weighting the argument. "He's got a good point, Mr. Tiebolt. I'm afraid you can't have it both ways. We will reconvene at the Dolphin Key Center for Dolphin Human Therapy tomorrow morning at ten o'clock, but Mr. Fontana will not serve as intermediary."

CHAPTER THIRTY-THREE

Just after dusk, Mike stood with Katy Grant on the far dock, leaning over the wooden fence rail toward the sea. A breeze had blown the heat out of the day and washed the fog toward shore: A damp gray mist, the same color as the sky, clung to the sea surface as if it had been painted onto the scene.

"Homer and I both figured we'd lose otherwise," he explained. "This was our ace in the hole."

"The two of you should have checked the rest of your cards before you flipped it. You should have known the judge might eighty-six you," Katy said, her stomach still in knots over Mike's suggestion that she take his place at tomorrow's demonstration.

"We did."

Around them, the mangroves shifted in the breeze, crackling icily.

"You should have said something to me first, then."

"What would you have said?"

"That I couldn't do it."

"That's why we didn't tell you."

"What about Gus? Can't he do it?"

Mike shook his head. "I'm the one who taught Sonny and

Cher the signals. You're the only other person who knows them."

"But I'm not ready to work the dolphins alone." The way the breeze blew Katy's mist-shrouded hair over her face made Mike think of her mother—his first wife—for the first time in a very long while. How beautiful she'd been, all the pain he'd caused, her funeral he'd learned drunkenly about two days after the fact. "I'd just make things worse."

Even Katy's voice sounded like that of her mother. Full of second chances beneath the makeup hiding her bruises.

"You didn't make things worse ten days ago when you told Homer Tiebolt about the trouble I was in," Mike said.

"I asked him not to tell you."

"He didn't have to tell me. I figure you were the one who told him about the lawsuit because you wanted to help."

Katy rolled her eyes. "I don't know what the hell must have come over me."

"I do," Mike said, without missing a beat. "You don't want to see this place go down the tubes."

"My time here is up in five months anyway."

"What about mine? And Joe's?"

"That's not my problem."

"I think it is."

"You've got a bad habit of being wrong."

"Not this time. Right now, Homer figures the odds of winning are fifty-fifty at best. If we don't go through with this demonstration tomorrow, that means Dolphin Key could be shut down the day after."

"What makes you think I care?"

"About me—I don't. But this isn't about me; it's about Joe and the dolphins and all of the people we've helped. We don't really get along too well, do we?" Mike asked her as the mist washed in over them.

"No."

"Except when we're working with a patient. Then something changes."

"So?"

"So that's how I know you can pull this off tomorrow. First I thought it was the dolphins you were different around. Then I realized it was more than that. The real Katy Grant is the one I see holding flash cards and buckets of fish and taking case notes, not the one who wants to make me pay for being the asshole I used to be."

"You forgetting about my track record?"

"Haven't you seen enough here to realize that track records don't count for a lot? Lots of people who pull into our lot are looking to start from scratch."

"You're talking about kids, coach."

"And their parents. Sometimes what's going on with their kids just tears them apart. So when we're treating the kids, we're treating the entire family. And when we open up a new world for a son or daughter, the same world opens for everyone in the household."

"Is that what you're trying to do for me? Because if you are—"

"I was thinking more like both of us," Mike told her.

Katy almost laughed. "Well, you've come to the wrong person if you're looking for me to save *your* world."

"You still want to hurt me?"

"Not particularly, and that's why I can't handle this demonstration tomorrow."

"But tomorrow's not just about me, it's about you. You've got to do this for yourself, because if you don't you'll be turning your back, walking away." Mike stopped to let his words sink in, watched Katy shudder a little as the mist wrapped around her. "Sound familiar, kid? You wanna follow in my footsteps? Turn around one day and see everything you turned your back on and can't have again right before you? You find you want it back, want to reach out and see what you can grab. Except it doesn't feel the same anymore." Mike lowered his voice. "Look, I know there's probably no chance for us the way I was hoping; maybe the baggage is just too heavy. But I'm not going to give up trying to make you realize the same thing about you that I already have. That's what tomorrow's all about. To prove you can do it. Give you the chance to make it for yourself, on your own."

"Speak my first word, something like that?"

"Close enough, yes."

Katy brushed the hair from her face. "You might live to regret this, coach."

Mike shook his head. "I don't think so. Not this time."

CHAPTER THIRTY-FOUR

The judge arrived with the clerk and court reporter at 9:45 the next morning, just before Arlan Moss and a tight-lipped Max Hollister. A crowd of noisy reporters and commentators had jostled for position at the wooden fence just up from the shoreline, until Mike asked the judge to order them and their cameras to the parking lot. That left only Mike, Joe, Jacardi Benoit, and Gus Anton as spectators.

A brief rain after dawn had left the concrete around the pen on Dolphin Key's far side dappled dark. The sun burned hot and hard and lifted a thin layer of steam from the splotches, bleaching them light again. Katy felt the sun on her shoulders as the court reporter placed a laptop computer on a plastic table that had been set up within easy earshot of those allowed to remain.

"Mr. Tiebolt," said the judge at ten o'clock sharp, "we are ready to proceed."

Katy looked once more at Mike. His face was emotionless, the sun framing it behind his shoulder. Joe stood beside him, the boy's shoulder pressed against Mike's chest. It was a pleasant shot, backlit by the sun in a bright blanket of hot light that splayed into the cool dark waters of the pen. Katy gazed at father and son and saw how much they needed each other, and today how much they needed her. She could feel the heat of the concrete through her sandals, her toes wet with a light coating of steam.

"If it please the court," Homer Tiebolt began, "I will now turn the demonstration over to Katy Grant, assistant trainer for the dolphins in question."

"Look," Katy began after clearing her throat, "I haven't really been here long enough to understand all the stuff that was discussed in court yesterday. I don't know a lot about dolphins, but we seem to get along pretty well, and I knew right from the start that they wanted to talk to us as much as we want to talk to them."

She stole a gaze up at Mike who nodded supportively.

"What you're about to see is a demonstration of a way we might be able to do that someday. Places like big centers and institutes that get all the big funding spend all their time recording what dolphins say and trying to make words out of it." Katy shook her head. "Uh-uh, sorry. Doesn't work that way. Much better to concentrate on teaching the dolphins to understand the way we talk instead."

"Your Honor," snapped a smirking Arlan Moss, "is this to be considered expert testimony?"

"Not at all, Mr. Moss. I believe we covered that yesterday. Ms. Grant is merely acting as a facilitator, not an expert."

Judge Rosenthal gave a slight nod, and Katy thought she saw a smile flicker briefly.

"Mike Fontana over there," Katy continued, glancing at Mike, "has taught the dolphins some signs, like for deaf people, and combined the signs with words to help the dolphins tell one sign from another. He could be instructing them to do something, or asking them a question they're supposed to answer. Mike calls it vocabulary building, a foundation on top of which everything else can grow."

As she paused to collect her thoughts, Katy realized her skin felt cold and clammy.

"You can't see it clearly from where you are, but attached to the side of this pen is a sixteen-station keyboard. The dolphins will answer questions that Mike—I mean, I—ask them by touching one or more of those stations with their noses."

She realized she was having trouble forming her thoughts into words. She wanted to call this off and run away before she made things worse.

"The keyboard is connected to a computer, which is linked to the loudspeaker directly behind me."

Katy turned to point out the speaker and banged into the tripod supporting it, nearly tipping the speaker over. Arlan Moss and Max Hollister covered their mouths to hide their laughter. Mike's expression hadn't changed. His eyes coaxed her on, but Katy could feel herself losing it right here for all to see.

"The computer turns the symbol the dolphin touches into a word that the dolphin, and we, can hear," she said, forcing herself to keep going. "That's how they begin to understand how our language works. And, at the same time, we record the sounds they make that we hope correspond to our language."

"Perhaps we should start by placing the dolphins under oath," interrupted Arlan Moss.

"That will be quite enough, Mr. Moss," scolded the judge.

"We must not stand for this!" Max Hollister cried out. "Bad enough to take a creature out of its world. But to try and indoctrinate it in our ways is the ultimate in disrespect, the ultimate in self-serving and pointless exploitation of an animal!"

"You are out of order, Mr. Hollister," cautioned Judge Rosenthal.

"No! It's this place that's out of order. What's happening here is the most dangerous threat to the long-term survival of a species in the wild I have ever encountered!"

"Right now, this place is to be afforded the same respect as my courtroom, Mr. Hollister," the judge said flatly. "Mr. Moss, please control your client or I will ask him to remove himself."

Hollister turned to glare some more at Katy, and she felt a familiar surge of anger building up inside her. Suddenly she didn't feel hesitant anymore. Suddenly she wanted to be here and only here to give Hollister what he deserved. Katy knew anger well, as a foe for all of her life but now, perhaps, as a friend. Turn the tables on the emotion that had carved out such sharp, unfinished edges in her life.

"Ms. Grant," Judge Rosenthal said, beckoning her to continue.

Katy felt a warmth overtaking the clamminess that coated her skin. She snapped alert, ready to call Sonny and Cher to her, when she saw they were waiting at the edge of the dock.

"I'd like to start off with something easy," she said to the members of the court assembled around the pen, but her gaze lingered briefly on Hollister. The familiar grip of anger tugged at her, hers to control, to use, and Katy started the proceedings by raising her right hand in the air. "Sonny, bring red ball!" Her left hand went into the air as the first dolphin sped away. "Cher, bounce blue ball!"

Katy watched as Sonny retrieved a red rubber ball from

the corner of the pen and pushed it back toward her, while Cher darted toward the blue ball in the opposite corner, drew it underwater, and began bouncing it against the concrete wall of the pen.

She blew the whistle and the dolphins swam back to her. Katy leaned over and tossed each one of them a fish from a bucket by her side, then stood up again. "That's just a small demonstration of their ability to follow more than one command in the same sequence, while they are asked to differentiate between colors at the same time."

"Your Honor," began Max Hollister before Arlan Moss could stop him, "may I be heard?"

"Quickly, Mr. Hollister."

"The fact that feeding was used to reinforce behavior indicates we just watched a trick, a performance."

"I'm fully capable of making such evaluations on my own, Mr. Hollister," the judge said scaldingly. "Are you finished?"

"No, Your Honor, I am not. A performance follows a sequence any animal can commit to memory and complete by simply repeating the steps without true awareness of what it is doing."

"Go on."

"I would suggest, implore, that you order the questioning process to begin now in order that this sequence be disrupted and the whole process exposed for the sham that it is."

Judge Rosenthal weighed Hollister's words without comment, nodding slowly. "I am inclined to agree. Mr. Tiebolt, are you ready to question your witnesses?"

Homer came forward. "I am, Your Honor."

"Ms. Grant?"

"Ready, Your Honor," Katy said and took a deep breath.

CHAPTER THIRTY-FIVE

"Question time!" Katy announced to the dolphins. She flipped each of them a fish while she awaited Homer Tiebolt's first question.

"Ms. Grant, could you please ask them if they are happy."

Katy raised her right fist into the air to signal Sonny. "Sonny happy?" she asked, signaling with her hands and arms. "Answer!"

The dolphin dove instantly and swam for the sixteen-station electronic circuit board encased in plastic on the near side of the pen. The touch of his nose to the board would automatically activate the segment behind the section of plastic. Stringing words together into phrases or even sentences required the touching of more stations in sequence.

"*Feel good,*" a computer-synthesized voice blared through the speaker, and Cher seemed to smile as Sonny resurfaced.

"I'm sorry," Katy said to Judge Rosenthal. "I asked him how he felt, not if he was happy."

Katy repeated the process, changing the signals subtly as she asked, "Sonny happy?"

The dolphin dove again and pressed a different part of the plastic over the circuit board.

"*Yes*" emerged from the speaker.

Katy raised her left fist in the air and focused on Cher, repeating the same sequence of signs as she said, "Cher happy?"

Cher sliced to the circuit board and seemed to inspect the panel briefly before making a choice.

"*Eat*" emerged from the speaker.

"Cher happy?" Katy repeated when she resurfaced.

Cher dove again and touched the identical spot on the board.

"*Eat.*"

"Your Honor," interrupted Max Hollister again, "the dolphin is simply stating what it wants, a conditioned response."

"Let's see," said Katy, as she fed Cher a squid and then asked the question for a third time after she swallowed. "Cher happy?"

The dolphin sliced below the surface, seeming to move faster than before.

"*Yes.*"

"Ask them," began Homer Tiebolt, "given the choice, if they would want to leave."

Katy gave Sonny a squid, just as she had Cher. The next signs were more complicated, and she went through them slowly.

"Sonny leave home?"

The dolphin didn't hesitate.

"*No.*"

He was cackling when he crested the surface, as if to emphasize the point.

"Cher leave home?"

Cher dropped below the surface, touched the board.

"*Friend.*"

Cher poked her head up and blew water from her mouth. Katy repeated the sequence.

"*Friend,*" the dolphin answered again.

"I think I know what's happening," Katy said to Judge Rosenthal. "She's telling us *why* she doesn't want to leave."

Katy threw each of the dolphins a fish.

"Can you ask them if they miss their old lives?" Homer wondered.

"I can try," Katy said. "Sonny, go big water?" she asked, pointing out to the ocean.

The dolphin was under like a bullet. "*No.*"

"Why?" Katy asked as soon as he resurfaced.

"*Me here*" came his answer.

"He can't say 'home'?" wondered Homer.

"It's not one of the options on the circuit board, not yet anyway." She signed the same question for Cher. "Cher go big water?"

The dolphin dropped below the surface.

"*Eat.*"

Katy fed her a fish and repeated the sequence of signs when she resurfaced. "Cher go big water?"

"*Eat.*"

One more time.

"*Eat.*"

"Your Honor," said Arlan Moss, "can we suspend this farce?"

"She's answering the question," Joe snapped angrily from Mike's side. "You're asking her if she wants to go back to the ocean. She's saying, like, 'Why brother?' She gets everything she wants here. All she has to do is ask."

"Your Honor, *please!*"

Judge Rosenthal stood there noncommittally. "Ms. Grant, is a dolphin capable of making such a cognitive leap?"

Katy gazed at Mike before responding. "That's what we're trying to find out, Your Honor."

Cher tossed some water at the judge with her nose.

"Mr. Tiebolt?" Rosenthal said, brushing herself off.

Homer turned spryly toward Arlan Moss. "Your witness."

Moss smirked, glad for the opportunity. He approached the pen as if it were a witness stand where his quarry awaited questioning with apprehension. But the dolphins regarded him casually, paying little attention.

"Miss Grant," Moss began sharply, treating her like the witness instead, "please ask the dolphins if they have ever been mistreated."

"I . . . don't know the signals for that question."

"You mean the dolphins have not learned those signals—or words—yet, don't you?"

"Maybe. I don't know."

"I'm sure you don't. Then could you please ask them if they are happier now than they were before when they were in the wild?"

"I don't know the signals for that either."

"I understand."

"We haven't gotten through the whole dictionary yet, like the word for—" Katy stopped herself from saying "asshole" just in time.

Moss snapped his head toward the judge. "Ask that the witness respond only to direct questioning, Your Honor."

"Your witnesses, Mr. Moss," Rosenthal corrected, "are in the water."

The lawyer's face puckered a little, breaking its statuelike flatness. "I stand corrected, Your Honor." He turned back to Katy. "Could you please ask them what circumstances led to them coming here?"

"I can't." Katy felt her face reddening, the heat building behind her cheeks.

"What about how they feel about being separated from their own species here?"

"I don't know, how do you feel about it?" Katy said, while before her Sonny and Cher waited expectantly for their next question. She tossed them each a herring to hold their attention.

Moss seemed to be waiting for Judge Rosenthal to say something but continued when she didn't. "What about if they miss the families they left behind?"

Katy shook her head. "Sorry."

Moss smiled at her, getting even. "No need to be. Your Honor," he blared triumphantly, "it would seem the only questions these dolphins are capable of responding to are those the defense has already trained them to answer."

A long moment followed where no one, not even the dolphins, made a sound, until Homer Tiebolt moved forward, looking both confident and determined.

"If it please the court . . ."

"Go ahead, Mr. Tiebolt," Judge Rosenthal beckoned.

"Mr. Moss, if you were interrogating a witness who spoke only Spanish, how would you do it?"

"Through an interpreter."

"And if this interpreter was unable to precisely translate certain idioms and expressions?"

"I suppose I'd have to rephrase. But that doesn't apply in a case like—"

Moss stopped when he saw Homer's smile, knowing he'd been had.

"The defense raises a good point," agreed Rosenthal. "I suggest you proceed with it in mind."

Katy watched Mike squeeze Joe's shoulder. He gave her a nod as Moss stammered through his next words before settling on what to say.

"Can you ask them where they were before?"

Katy signaled Sonny and did her best. The dolphin hesitated briefly, then rocketed under the surface to the answer board.

"Here" came his answer seconds later.

"I'm sorry," Katy said and flipped Sonny a fish.

"No problem," Moss replied, confident he was making his point. "Ask him if he would like to go home, back to the ocean."

Katy did and Sonny plunged downward again.

"Here," the computerized voice droned.

"I believe we just heard the same answer," Moss said. "Your Honor, apparently the dolphin is merely repeating itself."

"On the contrary, Your Honor," argued Homer Tiebolt, "I would suggest that the witness is simply making the point that this *is* his home, his *only* home."

"I would like to know how they feel about people," demanded an increasingly belligerent Moss. "I would direct the interpreter to ask the other dolphin how it feels about living among people."

Katy tossed Sonny a fish and focused her attention on Cher. "Cher like man?" she asked, mirroring her words with the proper signs.

The dolphin shifted in the water but didn't respond.

"Cher like man?" Katy said, repeating the signal as well.

The question must have clicked suddenly because Cher dove beneath the water like a bullet.

"*Eat him,*" the synthesized voice said, just before Cher soared out of the water directly in front of Arlan Moss, splashing the lawyer and clacking noisily.

Moss stumbled backward, nearly falling. Then, as if understanding the context of her own joke, Cher rode her tail backward, spun into the air, and surged underwater where Sonny joined her. Both quickly resurfaced in front of Katy who fed them gratefully.

"I couldn't have said it better myself," she whispered.

"Your Honor," Moss started to protest, wiping off his glasses, "hasn't this farce gone far enough?"

Judge Rosenthal came forward until she could look clearly into the pen. "I'm inclined to agree that it has, Mr. Moss, and I'm also inclined to issue my ruling here and now." She turned to address all those assembled. "This court finds there to be insufficient evidence under the federal Marine Mammal Protection Act to warrant a custodian being appointed to run this facility in the interim before trial. The complainant's motion is hereby denied."

Mike hugged Joe tight against him. Homer Tiebolt clenched his fists in the air. Katy tossed fish after fish to Sonny and Cher, who clung to the surface before her.

Arlan Moss seemed on the verge of lodging an objection when Max Hollister forced him aside, a bony finger thrust at Mike Fontana.

"You think this is over?" he challenged, his voice cracking.

"You think you've won? Not even close. I'm going to shut you down, Fontana! I'm going to shut you down, whatever it takes!"

"I would caution the complainant," Judge Rosenthal started. But Hollister had already sped past her, almost to Mike, who had his fists ready.

Suddenly Jacardi Benoit sliced between them. Hollister nearly bounced off the big Haitian's chest and found a reproaching finger being waved in his face as Jacardi's bulging eyes glared down at him.

"You know what, little mahn? Back home I got a doll look a lot like you. Behave yourself and act your age, or maybe I take your doll to the old ladies with the *gris-gris* so they can work the needles in the old way. You don't want to feel that, little mahn, you really don't. So leave now nice and quiet and I keep the voodoo magic away. Okay? And stay away from this place, or I stick the needles in myself."

CHAPTER THIRTY-SEVEN

They celebrated that night at Sunday's on the Bay. Mike, Katy, Jacardi, and Homer Tiebolt all had stone crabs, while Joe settled on a hamburger and Gus had some kind of fowl he relished every bite of, perhaps as revenge against the birds that continued to torment him.

"What about the trial?" Mike asked Homer Tiebolt over dessert.

The old man sat sideways in his chair with his legs stretched out straight before him. He chewed down his pain and fought to keep his mind sharp as the marker on the time he had borrowed over the last two days was called in.

"It'll never take place would be my guess," Homer said, springing alert. "And if it does, the results will be the same." He lifted his water glass in the semblance of a toast and battled his trembling hand. "We torpedoed them, Mike. We kicked them in the ass."

"And if Hollister didn't feel that," added Jacardi Benoit, smiling devilishly, "there's always the needles of the *gris-gris* women."

Mike laughed and turned toward Joe, who was finishing an uneaten slab of Homer's Key Lime pie. The lump on the boy's throat had definitely gotten smaller. Maybe just a virus—a cold or something this time. Maybe.

"Hey," Katy said to Jacardi, "you got room in any of your classes for me?"

The big Haitian's hand engulfed his entire coffee cup as he raised it toward his mouth. "I don't know," he replied and winked at Mike. "One Fontana's about as much as anyone can take."

Mike gazed across the table at Katy. "Looking for a permanent job?"

"With what you pay?"

"Sonny and Cher wouldn't know what to do without you."

Katy rested her chin in her hands and smiled. "I guess I'll have to think about it."

"Take your time," Mike told her. "I'm not going anywhere."

by
Scott Swaim
Director
Full Circle Program
Clearwater Marine Aquarium
Clearwater, Florida

I was not a strong believer in what dolphins can do for people, nor did I understand the bond that we have with them, until I experienced it for myself. I spent most of my adult life in the air force. During my military career, I was bouncing around the world on a giant C-5 Galaxy cargo plane, and it was a hell of a ride.

So how did an air force loadmaster end up working with children with special needs as well as dolphins, sea turtles, otters, and stingrays? Uncle Sam offered some great college benefits, and I started going to school to study psychology. After finishing my masters, my first real job was working at a shelter for runaway teenagers, and later with abused children in the foster care system.

One weekend, when I was driving to Clearwater Beach to get some sand and sun, I happened upon an open house at the Clearwater Marine Aquarium. I figured the beach could wait and made a U-turn to take a closer look. I had no idea of the large impact that U-turn would have on my life.

The small aquarium was populated by sea turtles, two river otters, and a mangrove exhibit. But it was a dolphin that caught my eye as I watched him jump, spin, and interact with a trainer. I listened to a volunteer tell the guests his story.

That dolphin is named Sunset Sam. He was stranded on a mudflat in old Tampa Bay back in 1984 and was rescued by the aquarium. Sunset was brought back to the facility in grave condition. He had pneumonia, pox virus, severe dehydration, and parasites. He was treated by the aquarium staff for over eighteen months. During his rehabilitation, it was also discovered that Sunset had liver damage and was visually impaired in his right eye.

I learned that the Clearwater Marine Aquarium was actually a hospital for injured marine animals. They treated sea turtles that may have been hit by boats, dolphins that were sick or injured, and even orphaned river otters. Before I left for the day, I decided to fill out an application to join the aquarium's volunteer force and came across a program called Full Circle. The brochure said it was an animal-assisted therapy program for special-needs children. Being a traditionally trained mental health therapist, I was skeptical about the "magical" claims often associated with such programs.

I couldn't have been more wrong.

I visited the following Friday to observe a session, during which I watched the program director and an intern work with a little boy who was born without legs. I was floored! This child was bouncing around, feeding Sunset Sam and the sea turtles with a smile a mile wide across his face. The director explained that since the boy's first session, he had finally come out of his shell and had really taken charge of feeding and caring for the animals.

That was three years ago. Both the aquarium and the Full Circle program have grown, and I now serve as the program's director. I have learned so much about how animals like Sunset Sam can enrich our lives, and how we can enrich theirs. Sunset brings to the therapy sessions not just a strong reenforcement that helps children achieve treatment goals but also a sense of balance and acceptance. Victor Frankl believed we have to find purpose in life, *to find meaning, that one thing that makes life worthwhile.* I found those roots and that meaning right here at the Clearwater Marine Aquarium. We try to help animals and children with special needs find some meaning and direction for their lives. We do not perform miracles, nor do the animals. We are just people helping animals and animals helping people.

Sunset Sam has helped many children with special needs and has done far more than his share of enriching people's lives over the years he has been here. . . . Yes, he really does paint and seems to enjoy it. Sunset's disabilities prevent him, for his own safety, from being released back into the wild. He is currently alone in his pool and we think he deserves a companion.

Finding a companion for Sunset is not the easiest thing to do, though. You can't just put an ad in the paper: *Single 20-year-old male Atlantic bottlenose dolphin seeks single female. I have my own place and plenty of fish so come over, see my paintings and have a few minnows!!!!* . . . and it promises to be very expensive.

But you can help us help Sunset. Sunset Sam and all of us at the Clearwater Marine Aquarium would appreciate any contributions you can make to the FIND A FRIEND FOR SUNSET SAM FUND.

Dolphin Key is fiction. But the contributions of Sunset =Sam and other dolphins in programs like Full Circle are anything but. If you would like to help us bring Sunset "full circle," too, please visit our web site at CMAquarium.org or contact us at the following address:

Full Circle Program
Clearwater Marine Aquarium*
249 Windward Passage
Clearwater, FL 33767
727-441-1790 ext. 21
email: fullcircle@cmaquarium.org

*AUTHOR'S NOTE: The Clearwater Marine Aquarium is a 501 (c) (3) non-profit organization that has been providing rescue and rehabilitation to marine animals for over twenty-five years.